ONE DOOR CLOSES

ONE DOOR CLOSES

by
Joyce de Brett

HERMES
2 Tavistock Chambers, Bloomsbury Way, London WC1A 2SE

ISBN 1 86032 025 2

Cover design and typesetting by Jim Barry

Made and Printed in Great Britain by M.B.C., Ipswich, Great Britain

THE LEISURE OF MAN'S FIRST DEATHLESS LIFE

(Legend of Jubal)

Man's life was spacious in the early world:
It paused, like some slow ship with sail unfurled,
Waiting in seas by scarce a wavelet curled:
Beheld the slow star-spaces of the skies,
And grew from strength to strength through centuries:
Saw infant trees fill out their giant limbs,
And heard a thousand times the sweet birds' marriage hymns.
Time was but leisure to their lingering thought,
There was no need for haste to finish aught;
But sweet beginnings were repeated still,
Life infant-babblings were that no task fulfil,
For love, that loved not change, constrained the simple will.

By George Eliot.

Chapter One

TO THINE OWN SELF BE TRUE

"To thine own self be true -
and it must follow as night
follows day, thou's canst
be false to any man."

Hamlet, Act 1, W. Shakespeare.

The above well-known phrase was said to me once. I have never forgotten it.

How many masterpieces of writing have been carelessly thrown aside, because the first page made no impact on the critic, but it is this very page which is the hardest to write. This book - no masterpiece naturally - is devoid of falsehood, and as I always endeavour to be true to my own self I can state that this book is based on truth. It is spiritual philosophy based on my own personal experiences of life. The only reason I have summoned up the courage to write this is because I hope this book will fill a need in someone's life who has undergone the same experiences as myself. Those who have hit rock bottom, and for whom each day is a depressing struggle, when the world presses around one, and it seems the sun will never shine again. These are the times when mere man seeks to understand a deeper meaning to life.

This book has been dedicated to my twin-soul, but I would like to thank a dear friend whose idea it was in the first place to write it, also to Dorothy White, who for five years lent her house to our little group, and especially to Florence Sporton without whom these meetings would never have taken place. It is to dear Florrie, a true and dedicated Christian (although she was quick to point out that she was a Christian Spiritualist), who regularly journeyed one hour by train to Dorothy's home in all weathers, once a fortnight, just to give comfort and advice and healing to those in need. Never in good health, but this never deterred her from making these visits. She kept this up for four years. Because however, she believed in psychic phenomena and healing, and was a marvellous clairvoyant and clairaudient, she was frowned upon by all the orthodox churches in her vicinity. This book, I hope, will show how wrong these churches are. I will now go right back to the beginning which brought the three of us together . . .

The liner, one of the oldest in the Union Castle Line was pulling away from the docks at Port Elizabeth, South Africa. As always the weather was perfect. A seething mass of people had gathered on the quay-side, seeing off friends and relations. Some had arrived just to say farewell to the liner, always an attraction whatever one's age. This time though was to be the old girl's last trip and after giving years of service, would be sold and broken up for scrap at the end of the voyage. The liner was festooned with streamers, balloons and other decorations the crew thought would cause laughter. A band was trying it's best to be heard on the quay amidst cheering and hooting of car horns as well as the deafening roar of the ship's siren! Most of the crowd were laughing and happy, but I noticed some were silent and crying due to a loved one departing perhaps, or maybe the thought of the great ship being sent to the junk yard was too much to bear. The crew would all have to find new positions, people cry for many reasons.

I was also crying, standing with my husband and four children on deck. We were one of the many families returning to the United Kingdom. My best friend and neighbour, Adelaide, together with all her family and friends had come to wish us farewell. What can one say at such times? Her children and mine had made friends from the beginning, and I had lost the best neighbour I would ever have. She was an Afrikaaner, married to a Scot, and it always amused me to hear her speak in Afrikaans and then suddenly in the middle of a sentence switch to English.

It was dusk when we finally departed, the ship's siren tearing us apart with its mournful wail. I have never felt so miserable. People on the ground were frantically waving to those on deck. We could just spot Adelaide and the others, and called and waved. The liner's engines had started. We stood there watching everything growing smaller, shivering in the night air in our summer clothing, looking wistfully at the lights of Port Elizabeth, knowing we would never return. Were we doing the right thing, I thought, leaving this lovely country. I turned around and everybody had left the deck leaving my husband and children still gazing out at the quayside where we had often waited the arrival of the big liners. The liner headed into the Indian Ocean. We left the deck quickly and made our way to our cabins. They were adequate but small. Stan had one cabin with the two boys whilst I shared the other with the girls. We had a table to ourselves and looking around I noticed many people around our age with young children. I was too wrapped up with my emotions to really enjoy our meal, although sumptious and beautifully presented. We were returning to a country we had not seen for six years.

It took a few days to become acquainted with ship life, but after we had passed Mossel Bay, where we were quite ill, we settled down to the luxury of the life, and did absolutely nothing. A rare thing for me. Stan and I had much to talk about, we had never had so much free time. We were returning home with our four children, Angela, Roger, Anthony and Louise, Angela aged eleven being the eldest. Our future looked uncertain. We had no home, and Stan was unemployed. The children's education was also a problem. To be confronted with just one problem was difficult, but here we had three.

Our decision to return to England was based on several important points. Firstly we weren't happy about the state of South Africa. We had lived out there six years, and sensed it wouldn't be long before things would get uncomfortable. An assassination attempt had already been made on the President, Mr Hendrick Verwoerd. There was smouldering resentment amongst the blacks at the easy life of the whites - or some of them - as many Afrikaaners were quite poor, even in the cities.

Secondly we didn't want to give up our British Passports which we would have to do if we became South Africans. If we decided to remain we would have been cast as aliens and would have to report regularly to the police. Thirdly, we both missed our families, and Stan's father was in poor health. We also thought it wrong that the children were growing up never seeing their grandparents. Ours were the only grandchildren. Family life meant a lot to me, and I didn't want our children growing up without the companionship of their aunts and uncles who had been very good to me when I was young. I felt they would be 'missing out' in many ways if we remained. Some people are lucky enough to return home each year for a holiday, but we could never afford that luxury. Lastly I felt I never really belonged to the country, although we loved the open-air life, the golden beaches, and endless sunshine and blue skies. It was at Christmas that my thoughts turned towards home, and I can remember so well one holiday we spent in Basutoland - renamed Lesotho - we were miles away from a town, and Stan turned the radio on at about 11 o'clock at night one Christmas Eve, and the lovely voices from the choir at Kings College, in England really upset me and I realised that I was very homesick. I even missed snow, and the children had never seen it! It would have to be a complete break. Once we had made up our minds there would be no going back.

These then were the three reasons for returning. To remain however, the advantages far exceeded the former. A partnership had recently been offered to Stan by the Director of the engineering firm he worked for. His salary would be trebled. A great temptation. The firm was small but thriving. He was in charge of a mixed crowd, natives from various tribes, a few English and Afrikaaners.

Firm friendships were also made with three families. A young South African couple, my Afrikaaner neighbour and dearest friend Adelaide and her husband Blossom, and an English family who left England a few months after us. They came from the north of England and their accent and quaint mannerisms appealed to us. The husband was Maurice, an engineer who was also employed in Stan's firm. We naturally had more in common with them, the former two families never having lived in England - or seen it. It always caused amusement that having taken so much trouble to leave England, we were still interested in what was going on and how the country was faring. Their troubles were still our troubles it seemed - after all, our families were there. I found out within a few months that one cannot entirely cut one's self off from one's country of origin. None of us agreed with the South African politics, and all voiced our opinions as to how we would run the country. Like most newcomers we thought we knew the answers. But this country was a land of many customs, tribes, and religions, and we were no nearer the answers the day we left. We all agreed though that the black man got a raw deal. I had never seen so much poverty at the poor end of the town. Ramshackle tin huts, hot in summer, icy in winter - no fresh running water - only that which seeped in the road after rain, which wasn't often. They had no hope, no future, no holidays. A very hard life with very little money. I thanked God many times that I wasn't born black. They were very musical, and we brought back some records of Miriam Makeba - who rose to stardom, eventually travelling to Britain and the States. She was discovered in Port Elizabeth where we lived. There is something about an African choir which is very nostalgic to me. You cannot confuse it with any other singing. It can be recognised immediately.

The weather was one of the main advantages in staying, and for Stan, an enthusiastic photographer, it was perfect. We were out every weekend. There was always something new. Such a variety of wildlife. We hoped the children would appreciate them when they were older. Stan bought a cine camera and edited his films . . .

But right now we were in the Indian Ocean and heading back to England. I had been dreaming and was woken by the ship's bell reminding passengers it was lunch-time.

Chapter Two

LOOKING BACK

To try and describe the beauty of South Africa in a few pages is impossible. This was a land of contrasts. Kirstenbosch, on the slopes of Table Mountain, Capetown, has been described as 'A Paradise On Earth - more valuable than the wealth of Solomon.' It is a botanists delight, with giant Protea's and over a thousand species of plant life. The birds too are dazzling, the Cape Sugarbird whose tail is three times that of it's body. The Black-backed Kite, and the charming little Oriole's (the brightly coloured birds of the thrush family) who enchanted us when we fed them in our own garden back in Port Elizabeth. One day in our garden I found a wounded Hoopoe, another beautiful bird with beautiful plumage and a crest. It is a protected species. I tried feeding it, but it died.

We had lived in South Africa for six years and hadn't seen one eighth of the country or places we had hoped to visit. It was always a question of time. We just didn't have the time to see all the places in the three weeks of Stan's vacation. The country is enormous. Holland, France and Germany could just fit into it.

If we had been on our own we could have done it easily as we would have flown. With four children, the youngest only two and a half, it was too much to expect and too expensive We much preferred to drive, that way Stan could take photos. We never knew what was around the next corner. We drove for miles once with an ostrich trying to keep up the pace only 20 feet away from the road. Stan spent pounds on films. We knew once we returned to the England we would never return, so wanted to film as much of the wild life as possible. Not only for us but for the children later on in their lives. It was family history, of much loved friends and places, which can easily be forgotten over the years. I took one film only when Stan was at work. It was the day South Africa became a Republic. There was a great procession through the town. I was there early, and stood right by the edge of the road as the trucks and floats slowly passed, bright with streamers and people dressed in the old fashioned costumes of the Voortrekkers. The sun was at it's best. I couldn't go wrong. The film was a great success. I had captured everything. The crowd jostling and laughing, the brightly coloured clothes of people of mixed races. Stan was delighted. He never thought I could take any films. With people pushing all around me the hardest part was just to stand still.

Our holidays were spent around Capetown, and at Addo, the famous elephant game reserve. There we watched, hardly daring to breathe as the great beasts with their offspring the size of great danes came slowly forward from out of the trees at dusk. They blended in so beautifully with the background that we didn't see them until they were almost in our view. They came nightly to eat the tons of oranges left by the wardens. The distance between them and us must have been about 30 feet and yet we didn't hear a sound!

Elephants are one of the most intelligent and loving of the animal kingdom and the cows make wonderful mothers. It has been known for a female to remain for up to three days beside her dead calf. There is also a great bond between all the herd. About a ton of leaves, bark and other vegetable matter is consumed in one day by one elephant. If left to themselves they can cause much damage to the environment, especially if farms are nearby, reducing the earth to a wilderness.

Over-population and starvation would occur. Nature has her own way of dealing with this crisis. So have the poachers, and the horrific way they have treated them is heartbreaking, even taking tusks from the young babies. A bullet well aimed by an expert marksman is a quick death compared to a herd slowly starving to death, which is what would happen if all the grassland were eaten. In the 1950's, when we were there, about two million of them existed in the whole of Africa. This has now been reduced by half, if the report I read was true. As we left the game reserve I felt very privileged to have seen these wild yet gentle creatures . . .

My arm was being shaken. I realised I had been asleep. We were in calm waters now and the ship's engines with the unchanging rhythm and the hot sun had made me drowsy. This was a luxury I missed on the way out, as I could never rest with the two children. Stan was pointing ahead.

"We'll be arriving in Capetown in about an hour, then we can stretch our legs, let's go to the cabin and get suitably dressed."

We were all excited at the thought of revisiting Capetown.

The liner was going to be six days in dock. This was good news, to be able to see more of Capetown. People going ashore and returning had to hand in passports. This meant waiting in the long queue before disembarking.

Capetown for many was the end of their journey. They had come to this beautiful city for their annual holiday. Some had come from as far away as Beira in Mozambique, and Lourenco Marques, East Africa. Cave lovers head for the Cango Caves, one of South Africa's natural wonders. There water has percolated through soft limestone, where over thousands of years a fantastic sight has been formed. Light is reflected from pinnacles of stalagmites, and icicles of stalactites create a fairyland scene. I did hear that a new cave had been found and named as the Cango Wonder Cave, which is far more dramatic, but as with all unusual and beautiful works of art - natural or otherwise - vandals have taken their toll, and some caves have been stripped of their most beautiful structure. It is said that these Caves had been found by accident by a Mr Hendrik Van Zyl in 1780, looking for his lost cattle in the foothills of the Swartberg range which consists of chasms, gorges and mountain passes, of which Swartberg Pass is the most spectacular.

Holiday makers who love forest and sea would visit the famous Tsitsikama Forest, which we visited one year. This lies between the Outeniqua Mountains and the Indian Ocean. This extraordinary forest grows right down to the sea, near a resort called Knysna, where many beautiful shells can be found on the beach. A hundred species of trees grow here, the most famous being a yellow wood which grows to a height of 150 feet. Elephants live here but are rarely seen. They are said to be the largest of their kind. On our last holiday Stan had driven through the night from Capetown, the children being asleep in the back of the car. As the miles sped by I sensed Stan was becoming tired. At my insistence he stopped, and immediately fell

15

asleep with his hands still gripping the wheel. We woke by the chill of dawn and realised that we were at Knysna. On checking our map I realised he had driven 300 miles without a break. It is so easy to become mesmerised by a long straight road at night, with no other light except from the headlamps of an occasional vehicle . . .

I was brought back to the present at Capetown by impatient passengers rushing towards the gangplank. After we had disembarked, Stan, I and the children sauntered around the harbour where there were fishing boats unloading varieties of fish. Crayfish is popular, and in great demand overseas. Another favourite, Snoek is caught in winter off the coast, and can be cooked, dried and salted. In the 1930's the Government decided the harbour was much too small for such a busy port, and decided to re-claim land from the sea. This was begun, and a huge task it proved to be. It was completed in the 1940's. It is now known as the 'Foreshore.'

We had some lunch and decided to climb the mountain. There are quite a few worn paths leading to Table Mountain. Also a cable-car. It is well worth the climb to see all over Capetown. When one sees what has been achieved in South Africa, it is truly amazing when one realises that it was only 400 years ago when the first few white men landed here in three small ships. A settlement was founded here by the Dutchman Jan van Riebeeck.

One of the most ambitious projects undertaken by the South African Government was the building of the Hendrik Verwoerd Dam on the Cape's north-eastern frontier near the Orange Free State. Water is like gold to the farmers in the arid countryside, so this was a Godsend. There was an assassination attempt whilst we were there on the life of the President Mr Verwoerd, he recovered, but died a few years later. We returned to the ship later that evening. The following day we made a visit to a favourite park, and Kirstenbosch, once the property of the Kirsten family. Well worth visiting are the early buildings built by the Dutch settlers known as 'Cape Dutch' - with gleaming white washed walls and curved gables. Jan Van Riebeeck built himself a fine house at Rondebosch. We visited the famous one at Groot Constantia built around 1692.

Next day, new passengers began to arrive, who we viewed with interest trying to guess their nationalities. One striking young blonde turned all heads as she tripped along on very high heels just managing to avoid falling flat on her face. Speaking to her later, to my astonishment she told me she was Spanish, from the North of Spain. I think she was the only single female on board unaccompanied. Most of the passengers were families returning home to the UK or holidaying in Europe. They were a decent crowd all told. In one of his books George Bernard Shaw once wrote that 'to meet people at their worst go on a cruise' - I wonder which ship he went on? Maybe though the stewards and staff had a different tale to tell.

As the liner was due to depart I stood on deck peering up at Table Mountain, and my thoughts went swiftly back to the first time I beheld it. That was six years ago. It never fails to impress . . .

It was almost six years to the day when Stan came home from work one night. He was a foreman in a munitions factory and sick of his job. Also there was no hope of promotion. Prior to that he had been in the British Army in Palestine for three years. During that time his wages were put aside. He loathed the army, but like thousands of other young men had been called up. He felt honour bound to return to the old place. He stuck this out for a few years, and then one night he returned from work saying, "I cannot stand this job any longer. If I could find a suitable post overseas would you come?"

I thought for a moment. It would be a new life. England was going through a dead time. Life was a struggle. I was also ready for a change. A new life overseas sounded exciting. The only overseas journey I had made was to the Isle of Wight.

"Yes, alright, if that is what you really want." I said. The friends I had known were all married and overseas in various countries. The following weeks Stan read all the vacancies for engineers. He replied to some but received no replies. Three weeks later he found a letter on the mat with a South African stamp. He eagerly opened it. A firm in Johannesburg required a manager for their engineering firm. His qualifications were accepted, but first he would have to visit South Africa House in London. A month's trial by both parties was agreed. Stan replied immediately. Could they give him three months in which to sell his house? Nine days later another letter came through the door. Stan could hardly contain his excitement. Yes, they would wait three months, but no longer. All references, credentials, qualifications had been sent and approved. This was where our nightmare began. We were put under enormous pressure in the following weeks. First the house was put up for sale, furniture had to be sold and bills and taxes had to be paid. My mother kindly offered us accommodation for Stan, Angela, aged six, Roger, aged three, and I, whilst the sale of the house was in progress.

The house was sold in eight weeks. Stan wrote to the firm. All that remained was for Stan to book our flights. We would have to pay our own fare as it was not a government position. We were very lucky that things had gone so smoothly. The children were a bit quiet and off their food. I was slightly worried, and hoped they weren't going to get colds, but was very worried when they started coughing and were unable to keep their food down. I dashed to the doctor's surgery, luckily only a few minutes away. He saw me immediately. I realised afterwards that I should not have gone because of other children, but I was panic-stricken. I was not surprised when he confirmed it was whooping-cough. I then explained everything.

"I'm sorry my dear but the children won't be able to travel by air, not for a while anyhow, the airlines wouldn't agree anyway," the doctor said kindly. I stumbled out of the doctor's surgery, my mind in a whirl. Stan would have to go - the firm were expecting him. I took the children home and started to prepare the evening meal, waiting for Stan to arrive home from work.

Stan was shattered when I told him, but I insisted he had to go without us. Would my mother still be willing to accommodate us with two children ill with whooping-cough? Yes, she would, and she did. We wrote to the airline and they confirmed what the doctor had said. It would be a few weeks before they could fly, but we could always go by boat. I dreaded the thought of travelling by boat for three weeks with two sick children. Stan and I talked it over that night, and reluctantly he agreed to travel alone, after all, he had given up everything for this post in South Africa.

The children were bad, and it was just as well my mother agreed to let us stay. Stan was due to leave the following week, and I saw him off at the station in London, not knowing when I would see him again, and feeling very low in spirits. I would have liked to have seen him off at the airport, but it was a long way, and it would have meant my mother looking after the children all day. They were coughing all the time, and it was not fair to place this extra burden on her. I wanted to book a passage straight away, but Stan decided to settle first, then we could arrange things. As things turned out, this was the best advice he could have given. It was a tearful parting. Stan said he would write as soon as he could.

The first few weeks were awful. I had no sleep at all with the children, and was up half the night. It was just as bad for them. The doctor said a sea-trip would be the best thing for them when they had recovered, and for me also.

Each morning I rushed into the hall when the postman approached. It was not until two weeks had passed before I received the first postcard from Nice. The plane had stopped the first night in the South of France. A few days later I received the second postcard, this time from Khartoum in the Sudan.

"Dear Joyce, still struggling along. Now at Khartoum. Am having difficulty with currency. Bought this card with Bob's East African shilling. Very hot here. Will send letter from Entebbe. Love Stan."

(Bob was Stan's younger brother, and just before Stan had departed for Johannesburg had given him one East African shilling, saying it might come in handy!) It was just sufficient to cover the postage. The postcard from Khartoum was of native dwellings in the Nuba mountains, Kordofan. A group of round huts with thatched roofs in rocky terrain.

The third card arrived three days later. This time from Entebbe with a few hastily scrawled words, and the final card was sent from Johannesburg.

"Dear Joyce, my address for the time being is Allandene Hotel, 51 Soper Rd, Berea, J'burg. Write soon. Love, Stan."

It was a good two weeks before I received the first letter. I had imagined Stan living it up in the big city, being free to wander around without a wife and two children dragging along. This however was far from the case. As soon as he had settled in at his hotel, he immediately located the address of the firm who had engaged him and was shown into the managers office. He could hardly believe his ears when told that the firm had tired of waiting and had employed another manager! I can only imagine what Stan must have felt like.

He said he exploded, and told them he had given up everything, his house and work, just for this job (and had paid his own fare). In the end he was given a job as a foreman which he accepted. He had no alternative, as he had to live.

Stan felt very bitter. What had he let himself in for? His fare from England had taken quite a bit out of our savings. He was in a strange country, with no friends, and certainly no one whom he could trust. He stuck the job for two weeks, and then one day he just left. He decided there and then that he had to find another engineering post - but this time as manager. He certainly had no intention of being a foreman.

He had held that position in England, that was one of the reasons for leaving. He had given up everything. The firm promised to hold the job open for him. His references were excellent. It seemed that they wanted his experience without paying for it. In the New Testament it does say that 'a labourer is only worthy of his hire' or some such words. Stan had even paid his fare from England and hotel bills. Most firms pay for the whole family. He paid his own, which we could ill afford. He had no scruples about walking out.

After scanning the newspapers and settling his bill at the hotel, he read of several vacancies in Port Elizabeth at an engineering firm. A manager was needed, and as it was by the sea it was an added attraction. He caught the next train from Johannesburg. On arriving at Port Elizabeth he booked in at a family hotel opposite the beach. By this time it was late afternoon, so he took it easy for the rest of the day. He was interviewed the following day. It was an English firm. They needed a manager immediately. He was shown around and after several hours discussion was told he could start the following week. This was a great relief as he had been under terrible stress, and the flying and long train journey had tired him. I received a letter six days later telling me I could now book a passage.

I booked a passage for the two children and myself, but it wasn't until three months later that I rejoined him. I had stayed at my mother's home all that time, and don't know what I would have done without her. She and my brother Victor saw us off at King George V Dock at Woolwich, which was very convenient for us all, being only a thirty minute ride by taxi. The day was cold, grey and drizzly. I felt cold and icy after leaving the taxi, with rain trickling down inside my collar. We kissed each other goodbye and I felt very emotional, not knowing what to say, I tried to be cheerful.

"We'll only be away a few years. Time will pass. You can come and see us for a holiday."

"You'll never come back once you've gone," my mother cried miserably.

"I'll write as soon as I can, and will write each week, and we will return, but we must go now."

We all felt miserable. My mother kissed the children once more and we climbed the gang-plank of the huge liner. At the top I turned to wave. Were we doing the right thing. We had sold our home, leaving everything familiar, going to a country we knew nothing about, with no relations or friends to greet us at the other end. Everyone had thought we were mad and had told us outright. Well, it was up to us to prove them wrong. Just then a steward arrived and carried our suitcases to our cabin.

I was surprised by the number of young mothers with small children on board. Most were going to Rhodesia, (as it was then called) some to Beira. One is lucky to find a companion on board who shares one's likes and dislikes. I wasn't that fortunate, but formed a close friendship with two women of similar age and experiences. We ate at the same table, afterwards meeting on deck. We all felt pretty jaded as we each had small children to cope with. I felt I needed a rest from housework and cooking. Angela and Roger were still coughing, but after a few days on deck looked much healthier.

The food on board was excellent, but I hardly ate. It was rough going in the Bay of Biscay. Angela was ill, and I was living on my nerves as I had no sleep whatsoever whilst living at mother's. Just a few snatches on and off during the night. I couldn't even relax now with two young children. One evening I crept up to the deck and looked up to the stars, just wanting to be alone for a while, when a steward approached, saying he was sorry to disturb me, but one of the children was crying in the cabin. Roger had fallen out of his bunk. That was the last time I left them alone.

Our first stop was Rotterdam. I had to let mother know that we were alright, so I went ashore to post a letter. I also needed to find a chemist to buy some cough-mixture. The weather was cold and bleak, and I was glad to get back to the warmth of the ship. The cabins were comfortable. We were now sailing into warmer weather and I was so grateful just to sleep and read on deck knowing we had another nine days in which to do nothing. Our next stop, St. Helena, was a small island situated roughly 1,000 miles due south of Monrovia in the horn of Africa. The weather became hotter and the three of us came out in a heat rash which caused great irritation.

One day I was sitting on deck reading. It was a beautiful sunny day with hardly a breeze. A cloud passed over. I looked up curiously and was startled to see a huge bird with a very large wing span. I thought it was going to land on the deck. One of the crew said it was an albatross. They are often seen at a great distance from land. I could not see its face, it had passed too quickly. Strangely enough, I had just read about the giant reptiles, dinosaurs and pterosaurs which dominated life on land, sea and in the air in the Cretaceous period, about 136 million years ago.

Two days later I went down with dysentery, together with a few other passengers and crew. I had no option but to remain in my cabin. My chief worry was the children. A steward kindly looked after them at meal times. Who would look after them the rest of the day? Somehow things worked out well as they played with the children of my new found companions. The ship's doctor examined me and the children, advising me to eat nothing, but to drink plenty of fluids. He saw that I was very thin, so I had to explain this was due to the fact I had little rest the past month, and had very little food during the voyage. The second day I felt hungry, yet when the steward brought me a boiled egg I could not eat it. I felt awful and only hoped I would be over it before I met Stan at Port Elizabeth.

The sun was just coming up when the ship arrived at Capetown. I felt better that day and went on deck, as everyone did, to see the mountain. The most dramatic view of Table Mountain is undoubtedly that which is presented to travellers approaching Capetown by sea. It really is flat like a table and shrouded in mist and is quite breath taking. This was the first time I had travelled abroad. Passengers were allowed to go ashore, so my two companions and I spent a few hours in the city which was so completely different from London. I was struck first by the cleanliness of the docks, and the sun shining on the white buildings against the blue sky and patches of green grass. So unlike the docks of London, it seemed like another world. Once in the town we were all totally unprepared for the profusion of colour, of bright clothing, different styles of dress and coloured faces of mixed races. Adderley Street was famous for its flower sellers, and the dazzling colours, red, orange and golds were really a sight for travellers sore eyes. Colours were everywhere, even on the nearby beach at Bloubergstrand where small red Mesembryanthemums were dotted - known there as 'vygies.'

To the three of us it was like coming to another planet. Summer clothing everywhere. No dark suits or bowler hats, hidious things. The sun was so warm it cheered us all. I could not help but compare it to my last morning in London. I wondered if it was still raining! How could anyone be depressed in this lovely country.

The auctions at the quayside were conducted in boisterous mixtures of dialects and languages I couldn't understand. After looking at the waving of hands and shouts in the crowd, I doubted if I was the only one. Time was going by quickly and we had to leave this riotous scene and make our way back to the ship, where the passengers seemed dull compared to the people we had just mixed with. I was amused at the way small babies were carried on their mothers' backs, and marvelled at the way they managed to stay there as they were swaying from left to right and bobbing up and down every time their mothers bent down or turned around quickly. I noted immediately the absence of prams, and realised how close to each other mothers and babies were. I didn't see any babies crying. They were certainly more content than babies in England. It was very hard on the women to have to carry a child for hours. I never saw a man carry a child as some fathers do in England.

Back on the ship I realised with a shock that in forty eight hours I would be reunited with Stan. I started sorting out clothes for the children. I wanted him to see them in their new coats then decided that if it was as hot in Port Elizabeth, as it was today in Capetown, the coats would be totally out of place. So I found something more suitable for them to wear.

It was six o'clock in the morning when Stan came bounding into the

23

cabin. He looked very brown and fit - and younger. He kissed us all, then drew back and looked at me.

"My God you look awful."

After not having seen him for three months I wondered what his first words would be, but wasn't prepared for this.

"You should have seen me when I was ill," I joked.

This broke the ice and we laughed. I quickly explained, and also told him I had to settle up the doctor's bill. After bidding farewell to my two companions, who had another two more days on board before joining their husbands, we left the ship which had been our home for nearly three weeks and stepped once more on dry land. The ship's crew had been magnificent. So this was Port Elizabeth. This was to be our new home. We had spent nearly all of our savings on fares and had travelled half way round the world. I hoped we had done the right thing . . .

That was six years ago, and here we were on another ship heading back to England. I had been gazing up at Table Mountain and the thoughts had come flowing back to the time when I had first beheld it from the sea. The usual tears and hasty goodbyes, but this time no one was seeing us off, but we were just as affected by the departure. It was a beautiful country. Would we ever return? Perhaps the children would want to visit it, especially Anthony and Louise who were born there. The many films Stan took would arouse interest. The liner was pulling away now, but this time into the Atlantic. Goodbye Table Mountain, and thank you South Africa for a wonderful six years.

> *'Tis hard to part when friends are dear*
> *Perhaps 'twill cost a sigh, a tear;*
> *Then steal away - give a little warning,*
> *Choose thine own time;*
> *Say not goodnight, but in some brighter clime*
> *Bid me "Good-morning."*

From 'Life' by Mrs Barbauld.

And so ended a chapter in our lives. The future looked uncertain, and I wasn't looking forward to it.

Chapter Three

ARRIVAL

We were nearing Southampton and were standing on deck. We had arrived. Looking at the sky I could have been transported back in time. The sky was as I had left it six years ago. It was grey, even the rain was the same, a thin drizzle. Strange as it may appear, there were times when I would have welcomed it in South Africa. When it did rain it was a luxury. Sitting in our garden with the temperature well above the nineties in the summer. I even grew nostalgic when a letter arrived from my mother saying how lovely it was in England with the frost on the trees, and a light covering of snow. Oh well, we would experience this soon enough I imagined.

We disembarked. With Stan leading we made our way to the Customs Official. He went up to the officer. They seemed to be talking for quite a time and I sensed Stan was becoming agitated. I went up to them.

"Anything wrong?" I asked, looking at both of them. A silly question when it was obvious there was something very wrong.

"They want a receipt of course," Stan muttered.

"A receipt for what - that we've arrived in one piece," I joked.

Stan gave me an exasperated look. I didn't hear what he mumbled.

"They want a receipt for the camera I bought in South Africa, and any equipment bought. Do they think I'm a spy or something, as if I havn't enough on my mind."

"But you bought the camera five years ago. Why do you have to show them receipts?" I was becoming agitated now.

"Because that's the law - if they think it is new it has to be declared."

"But it isn't new."

"That's why they want proof and I can't give them proof. I don't suppose you have the receipts anywhere?"

This was so funny that I couldn't help laughing.

"Do you think I have had them in my handbag for five years without noticing them?"

"Well for my sake pretend to look through your handbag. I might have to pay customs duty and I don't want to do that."

I obliged, but by this time the Customs Official was being waylaid by other irate passengers annoyed at the hold up. He let us go, obviously believing it a waste of his time. Our first words on British soil and it ended in an argument because of red tape. Welcome home! Stan hired a car and driving through the Hampshire countryside I forgot how many greens there are in England. It was so beautiful, and coming up for autumn there were the usual golds and yellows.

"What was that sign?" Stan asked.

"I didn't see the first words, but the second was Chippings."

"Okay, keep on looking."

I looked behind, but we had turned a corner. My mother knew we would be returning that day. We continued about five miles without seeing anyone or any signposts. Stan thought he might be on the wrong road, and decided to go slower so as to get a better view of any sign. The last sign I had seen was a long way back.

"This is a long village," said Stan.

A couple of miles ahead we saw another broken sign lying by the road. We stopped and I read it.

"It is the same name?" I said.

"What does it say?" said Stan.

He wanted to get to my mother's house before darkness, not wanting to stay in a hotel without any English money, also he had made arrangements to contact his old bank as soon as possible.

"It says Loose Chippings," I said. "There you are, you can see for yourself.

"Where is the sign?" said Stan.

"It's fallen on the ground," I said.

Stan looked at the sign, looked at me incredulously, and then shook with laughter.

"What's the joke?" I said.

"You're the joke," he said. "It isn't the name of a village but a sign where the local councils leave gravel etc, to be used when required."

"Oh well, it's an easy mistake to make," and I read the other names I had seen on the map. Chipping Sudbury. Chipping Campden, Chipping Norton. One can imagine the amusement or annoyance it must cause motorists new to the country. After all, we had been away six years. I never did live that down. We even saw a sign marked 'North Pole.'

We were relieved to arrive at my mother's house, four hours later, to find my brother Victor cleaning his car. He hadn't changed. Mother had never seen either Anthony or Louise as they had been born in South Africa. She looked tired, after all she was putting us up for a while and had to do a lot of preparation. I introduced Louise (two and a half) and Anthony (four and a half) to their grandfather (Stan's father) and my mother. Here, a quick explanation is needed. My father had died in 1942 and my mother had re-married two years later. Her new husband had two sons and I married the eldest. So my husband was also my step-brother and his father was my father-in-law and my step-father! This was very convenient for us as we were all under the same roof, which saved us the trouble of driving from one grandparent to the next. My aunt Lily also lived in the next house but one. In fact it was Aunt Lily who had introduced my mother to Stan's father. She had also introduced Stan to me.

Stan's father looked frail. In fact when I had last seen him I thought I would never see him again. They made a fuss over the children- who were on their best behaviour. They all commented how brown and fit we were. We all retired late that night. Although Stan and I had each written a weekly letter to them, there was still a lot we hadn't told them. We had to make up for six years.

The following day we discussed plans. The first thing was a job for Stan. Then we would find a house. Angela and Roger would attend the local school. This was only temporary as we had no intention of staying in that area. We wanted to move to the country.

Whilst we were in Port Elizabeth, Stan had written an article for an engineering book, and had received some money for it. Also in the book were vacancies for engineers, teachers, etc. Before we left Port Elizabeth he had noticed an advertisement for a College Instructor, to teach young men at a college run by a paper group in Aylesford. They needed a qualified engineer, also one to teach trigonometry.

One Door Closes

In the first two weeks alone Stan travelled several hundred miles, all along the south coast. None of the vacancies or salaries appealed to him. He then remembered the advert in the engineering book in Aylesford. Aylesford was only one hour by train from my mother's home. If it was suitable it wouldn't be too far for her to visit us. The advert was now a couple of months old, but Stan went along. The building was new, near country surroundings with a monastery nearby. He was interviewed by the Head of the college who seemed amazed that Stan had seen the advertisement in a book in Port Elizabeth, some 6,000 miles away. He showed Stan around the college and explained the work that was to be taught. He seemed satisfied, and wanted Stan to start as soon as possible, as the other instructor would soon retire. When Stan explained he would have to find a house nearby, the Head explained that a new housing estate outside the village was being built.

We did find a house on the estate. It was the show house, the first built. It was not until three months later that we moved in, due to many delays. Meanwhile we had to continue to live at my mother's. This entailed Stan travelling by train every day. We moved into our new house in February 1961, and the children attended the local school which was at the end of our road. Our three greatest worries had been solved.

28

Chapter Four

A NEW LIFE

He who wintry hours hath given,
With the snow gives snowdrops birth;
And while angels sing in heaven
God hears the robins sing on earth.

Anon.

To us it was a cold winter. I went down with the flu, the first time I had suffered from a cold or bronchitis for six years. There were robins in the garden which cheered me up, but no snowdrops or any spring bulbs as we had only moved in. The garden could wait. It was a new house after all.

The children had now settled in their new school, and Stan was happy in his work. The Arch-deacon of the village church called on us the first week we had moved in, so from the start we felt that we belonged. Roger, the eldest boy, derived much pleasure from bell-ringing, which boy wouldn't, except one small boy who didn't let go of the rope and sailed up in the air! Angela, the eldest girl, and Louise were in the church choir. We were very happy in our new home, but how we missed South Africa. The average temperature for this time of the year would be about 69 degrees Fahrenheit at sea level. A Christmas card from Adelaide with flowers of the veld, brought home to us it that it would take a long time to get that beautiful country out of our systems.

The sun though wasn't too far away, and the following year Stan said we could spend our holiday in Spain, where to my surprise it sapped all my energy, and we all had to have a sleep in the afternoon, quite foreign to me. I could cope with the heat in Africa but not on the Costa

Brava. And those who have lived in Africa can never forget the immense velvet sky - so dark, together with a myriad of stars, and yet standing one night in the desert-like region between Pamplona and Zaragoza, we could see no difference, but only feel the very warm air, which could be quite chilly at night in Port Elizabeth close to the ocean. Spain was where we usually spent our holiday each year. One year we drove to the highlands of Scotland, and it took my breath away. God has been very fair I think, as there is something of beauty in all countries. Although a sun worshipper, it can make one feel languid, and is also annoying when one only has a limited amount of time for a holiday to have to abandon sight-seeing because it is too hot for walking.

The years were rolling by, all the children had left school except Louise who decided she wished to learn photography. Angela was a student-nurse, Anthony was studying electronics and Roger was working for a travel firm.

In 1973 Angela married, a few weeks after Princess Anne I remember, and decorated the church with pink crysanthemums. Her husband Richard came from the Midlands. He was a surveyor, blunt and straightforward. We liked him and his family.

We saw our families and relations quite often. One weekend we invited my mother down. It was the beginning of February. A warm spring day, very warm for that time of the year. We took her through the village up the hill towards the standing stones, called the 'Countless Stones' as one could never quite count the exact number. They were large megaliths reminiscent of the stones at Stonehenge, and at Carnac in Western France where we once walked through a long avenue of them.

It was just as we were crossing the road, from the stones to the field opposite, that a feeling came over me which I had never encountered in my life. I was in the middle of the road, at the junction, and I suddenly felt myself pulled down through the earth. I went icy cold and felt faint and very uneasy. What did it mean? I never told my mother or Stan. After five minutes the sensation vanished, but I have never forgotten that. We returned home to tea, it had been a beautiful weekend. Mother caught the train home later in the evening.

Chapter Five

FOREBODING

One adequate support for the calamities
of mortal life exists - one only;
an assured belief that the procession
of our fate, however sad or disturbed,
is ordered by a Being of infinite
benevolence and power.

'The Excursion' by W. Wordsworth.

It was the following Tuesday, 12th February, that I went shopping in
Maidstone. A ghastly day with torrential rain. The family had all left.
Stan had left at 8.15am. I passed an ambulance in the village, later
thinking it would be called out a lot in this weather. When I arrived
in the town wooden platforms had been erected over the pavements.
The River Medway running through Maidstone had burst its banks
and there was flooding. I had never known it to be so bad. I quickly
bought fruit, vegetables and fish for our evening meal and after
queuing in the open market was thoroughly wet so decided to return
home.
It was just after midday when I returned to find my neighbour Peggy
standing at her door. I waved to her, but she called me over.
"Joyce, please come in, I have something to say to you."
She looked pale.
"What is it, what's the matter?" I said, feeling a little frightened. She
looked shaken and started to cry.
"There's been an accident, the police have been here."
"Is it your husband, Peggy?" I said.
"No, it's Stan. The police called at your house but you were out. They

are coming around. They asked me to phone them when you arrived home."

I felt sick.

"Is he . . ."

"I don't know," said Peggy.

She looked as if she had been crying. She made some tea and brought me some. I was shaking so violently I couldn't keep the cup on the saucer, she took the saucer away. Another neighbour came in at the front door to see if any help was needed, but then left quietly. Fifteen minutes later a policeman and policewoman arrived. He didn't mince his words.

"Are you Mrs de-Brett?"

"Yes." I could hardly speak.

"Does your husband own a Vauxhall Viva?" he said, reading out the registration number.

"Yes," I said, not wanting to hear what he was going to say. I had been sitting when he came in. I tried to stand and nearly fell over. I felt myself shaking.

"I'm very sorry madam, there's been an accident, a fatal accident."

I clutched onto Peggy's arm, nearly fainting.

"Would you please come with us to the hospital for identification."

"What now? I can't come alone, could you please get hold of my son Roger who works near the hospital?" I cried desperately.

"Yes of course madam."

I felt myself beginning to sway but the policeman wanted some answers which brought me back to my senses.

"I will want to know the name of your son's firm and the address, then I will get a car to bring him to the hospital."

They were waiting for me to get into the car. I turned round to see Peggy who was wiping her eyes.

"Louise will be coming home from school soon," I said.

"Will you . . ."

"I'll watch out for her and bring her over here, don't worry about her."

Peggy couldn't come with me to the hospital as her children would also be arriving home from school.

We arrived at the hospital. Roger was waiting on the steps looking

32

very white. I couldn't speak, and we were ushered in to a small chapel. Roger went in first, looked at his father. then rushed out again. I made my way slowly, not knowing what I would see. Stan was covered with a blanket. I could only see his face. So pale. I kissed him. Perhaps he wasn't dead, doctors have been known to make mistakes. The policewoman had come in behind me and was holding my arm. I stood for about five minutes looking at Stan. She made no attempt to pull me away. I turned around and saw she was crying. What a rotten job for a young girl. She looked no older than nineteen. I was led to an office and handed Stan's clothes. I saw there was blood on his shirt. I signed some papers and then Roger and I were taken home.

I felt worn out, but had to prepare the children's tea. Louise came home a bit later from school. Roger broke the news. She looked stunned. A knock at the door brought me to reality. It was the doctor. Someone had told him. He said he could come back later that evening and give me an injection to help me sleep, and told me to try to eat something.

Anthony, now eighteen, arrived home late. He was completely devastated. Louise was now sixteen, both so young to be thinking of death. How would we cope without Stan, I could not imagine. He was the one who coped with all the money problems and difficulties, (but Roger stepped in and was a great help - although only twenty-two). The meal that evening was a silent one. I was thinking how Stan's death would affect us all. Certainly no more holidays for a while. It was ironic that on the morning of Stan's accident I had contemplated looking through holiday travel brochures in town, bringing them home and eagerly scanning them with Stan in anticipation of a nice holiday later, but the weather being so foul that day did nothing to put me in a holiday mood.

As promised, the doctor arrived at 8pm and gave me the injection, advising me to get to bed immediately before it wore off. This I did and within minutes felt groggy, hardly able to stand. I remember saying before getting on the bed, "Don't leave me Stan."

The distant murmur of voices woke me after midnight. Angela and her husband Richard had just arrived from their home in Gloucestershire, both shocked and tired after their long journey.

They had been married only three months before. As Angela entered my room it was then I cried for the first time. She must have witnessed many such cases being a nurse, but even this doesn't prepare one for a family tragedy. They stayed the night but both had to return to Gloucestershire the following day as Angela was on duty, having to put her own troubles aside looking after other folk perhaps in similar circumstances. They would be returning for the funeral. I still do not know who arranged the funeral - being in such a state of shock. Many people forget this, thinking it can be overcome in a few days, but it took me a month before I could even begin to think clearly again. Perhaps this is one of Nature's ways of giving the mind a rest.

Flowers for the funeral arrived immediately after breakfast. Some had left bunches, some wreaths. All beautiful spring flowers. As I had no flowers in my home I kept a beautiful container of miniature daffodils and deep blue grape hyacinths. Maybe they should have gone on the ground where Stan was but as Stan was cremated I didn't know where he would be. Anyway I thought, my house was still his house and he would have liked me to have them. It lifted my spirits just to see them whenever I entered my lounge. I cannot understand why people don't give the widow flowers, she needs them more than the deceased. I don't know how I got through the service. Before leaving the house I had a large glass of brandy to warm me up. It was a chilly day and I insisted the other mourners have some also. I still couldn't believe he was dead, and had a feeling that he must be somewhere in the universe. If he was, then he must be feeling bewildered and lost. I actually ended up praying for him, as we both needed help at that time. The service left me cold. I had no emotion whatsoever. Why can't the funeral service be a bit more cheerful. It would help a lot if the vicar were to say, that where there is true love God will never separate husbands and wives. Perhaps he did and I was in a world of my own. I was thankful when it was over.

Angela and Louise helped to prepare lunch. We tried to think of all the happy times. Stan's younger brother was very upset. I only wished his father could have been there. Relations offered to drive him. Perhaps he was too upset. All I know is that from that day he never mentioned Stan's name again.

A week later I was reading the local paper and there in large print was the headline, 'Lorry brakes fail on hill and motorist dies.' Yes, it was the fault of the lorry driver, and his second accident in one week. In a statement made to the police he said that he changed down into third gear as he went down the hill, and then found his footbrake wasn't working. He tried the emergency brake, this wasn't working either. His speed was about 15 mph. He said he saw a left-hand bend and decided to go across the road. He then collided with a red Vauxhall Viva car on the front-offside and it was pushed sideways. He then said he got out of his lorry and put out a fire which had started in the car's engine. At least he had tried to help Stan, I thought, but he never should have cut in front of him on that steep hill. He was obviously panic stricken, and had taken the easy way out, not thinking of the other motorist.

The accident had happened near the 'Count-less Stones.' My mind went back to the last time I was there. It was the day my mother and I crossed that road to look into the field opposite. When I remembered that I suddenly froze, as it dawned upon me that the place where the accident occurred was the exact spot where I had experienced that terrible sensation of being drawn down into the bowels of the earth!!

Chapter Six

GRIEF

True form - Spirit. Grieve not for one who is lost, grieve more for yourself, that you havn't learnt to see them in their new form. They are so often around you. Death cannot take them from the surroundings of those they love.

By Mentor.

Jesus said, "If thou canst believe, all things are possible to him that believeth." (St Mark, Chapter 9, Verse 23). Yes, I did believe, I am sure I believed that I would see Stan again, but as no one had ever told me that they had seen a dear one after death, how could I believe. I wanted proof, or something that would give me hope.

Can anyone see another's woe, and not be in sorrow too I wonder, and yet it seemed to me that no one really understood how I got through those few months. I wanted to die. It was only the thought of my children needing me that made me reluctantly rise from my bed each day. I discontinued the sleeping pills which my doctor prescribed. My will is strong, but even so, I knew that once I relied on them I would not be able to stop myself. Every morning was a dreary nightmare. I hated the new day. The snowy white pillow uncreased next to mine was a constant reminder.

"Oh, dear Stan, why did you have to go."

But if he were somewhere in this vast universe then he must be uttering the same thing. No one saw my falling tears. It was too personal a thing. And yet a plan was forming, as just three weeks before Stan's accident, I received a sad letter from Vivienne, an A.T.S. (Auxiliary Territorial Service) friend of mine. Her husband Don had died in the street from a heart attack whilst on his way to work. I wrote immediately to her offering my sympathy. Vivienne, Don and I had met in a mixed camp in Dalkeith about twenty-five miles south east of Edinburgh. There were soldiers, A.T.S. and some German and Italian prisoners-of-war. It was cold in the winter, and all the girls in our hut ended up in sick-bay with chest infections and colds. During our lunchtimes we went out in the nearby woods to collect wood for a fire in the evening. Don was a pleasant person with a kind word for everyone. I went out with him once for lunch, but mostly we all went out in a crowd.

I wrote to Vivienne immediately after Stan's accident. We had so much in common now. We both knew how the other felt. No one can possibly know until they have been through the same experiences. It is totally devastating.

People say my religion must have helped me. It should have but didn't. This not only angered me but surprised me. One needed it, especially in a crisis. So where was this help supposedly coming from one's religion? Deep down I'm almost sure I believed I would meet Stan again - but if only I could be certain.

In March that year there was a huge air disaster, three hundred and thirty-six killed in a DC10 on French soil. I realised this was a daily occurrence and heaven (if there was such a place) must have a constant stream of people queuing up. Every day people were dying. And where was Stan now? If I should enter the celestial spheres, what would I say? I had visions of myself enquiring, "Excuse me, have you met a fairly tall, slim man, aged fifty, but doesn't look it, named Stanley de-Brett, well read, highly intelligent, a fine face, sensitive personality, blue eyes, quiet manner, was in the Arab Legion, hobby photography, lived in Kent before passing to your side on 12th February 1974? A war film I had seen had made a great impression on me. It was about life after death. The scenery was wonderful. It showed a great multitude of people who had passed over, and how friends who had died in battle were re-united. A great comfort to those left behind. But where would I start amongst the multitude which no man can number. Would it be possible? I grew tired of being continually told to have faith. I did have faith, but in whom? I was brought up to have faith in God, and I knew it was through my prayers that my daughter was cured of polio when she was completely paralysed. I realised that I didn't have enough faith in my Church. Whenever I discussed death and the 'next world,' our vicar used to side-track the question. No one even discussed Stan after his accident, as if he were now on another planet, and was something to be pushed out of one's memory. How can one talk to and live with a soul-mate for twenty five years and then be expected to dismiss him from ones mind.

It was the nights I most dreaded, and would cry for hours. My thoughts went back to that first night directly after Stan's accident when I had asked him not to leave me. One evening, (which I shall remember for the rest of my life) I was in a deep sleep, warm and comfortable, when suddenly it felt as if the sheets on the bed were violently ripped off, and a heavy hand was shaking me violently by the shoulder. You would naturally expect me to be terror-stricken but I wasn't. Startled yes, yet knowing instinctively maybe Stan or some relation was trying to get through to me. Yet Stan didn't have a heavy hand like the one that woke me. Perhaps they had to shake me hard to get through to me. I sat up and said, "Is that you Stan?" and then went off to sleep again.

I awoke next morning and knew that I had to visit the local library. A voice seemed to urge me to go. So after breakfast I went. I walked around, not knowing what I was looking for. I walked around the Religious and Philosophy section, and stopped. A powerful force seemed to lift my arm high up on the top shelf to a book within my grasp. I picked it up and read the title. It was 'The Other Side' by a Bishop Pike.

I returned home, had a quick lunch and then settled down to the book. I would have a few hours before the children came home for their evening meal. 'The Other Side' is about a Bishop's son who committed suicide because he didn't think he would pass his exams and didn't want to disappoint his father. After his death strange things happened in the Bishop's flat. Objects would disappear and then reappear in unexpected places, and other unaccountable happenings. The Bishop, at length, decided to visit a medium in London by the name of Ena Twigg. He must have been unnerved, as the Church doesn't allow this. However, it was the Church's Fellowship for Psychic and Spiritual Studies who supplied him with her name. The Chairman being a Dr. Martin Israel. Mrs Twigg arranged for him to visit her at her house. She had asked that he bring an article along which had belonged to the son - something he liked very much. She confirmed that he had indeed taken his own life, and was sorry for the things which had happened in his father's flat, but that was the only way he could get through to him. He was sorry his death had caused his father so much pain, but he knew if he didn't pass his exam it would also give his father pain. Others in the spirit world had helped him to 'cause' those things to disappear and reappear. He knew in the end his father would try and find the cause, finding a logical solution.

Many other Bishops I am sure would have thought twice, as contact with the dead was not only unthinkable but unheard of. On the other hand, if they could be contacted then they couldn't be dead!! Anyhow, his love for his son was stronger than his love for his Church. He emerged from the medium's house a new man. I only hope he included his findings in his next sermon. He did however write a book, and if I had not read it I wouldn't have taken the steps I did. The book filled me with amazement. He wrote about psychic phenomena, and it must have been this which I experienced that night when my arm was shaken. It dawned on me that Stan was urging me to contact the same people. I was determined to find out the address of the Fellowship and see the Chairman.

I felt as if the Bishop and I were travelling along the same path. We had both suffered a terrible loss. Both believed in the Church. Our religions were identical. Most important we were not frightened to investigate.

Not for the first time I realised that if someone wants to do something, is determined enough, then help always comes. This came to me when a friend from my church called to say a lecture was being given the following week in Maidstone at a hall and anyone could go free of charge. I asked what the lecture was about. She thought it was about philosophy. I replied that I wasn't interested. She then said that I hadn't been out socially since Stan's death and it was about time I did. Just to please her I agreed to go with her and a few others. You can imagine my surprise when entering the hall to hear that the Chairman of the Churches Fellowhip for Psychic and Spiritual

Studies was present and would be speaking that night. I was sitting in front and so listened carefully. At the end of the lecture when people had gone home I approached Dr. Israel and told him everything, Bishop Pike's book and Stan's death, and if the Bishop had managed to contact his son could I not contact my husband? He looked at me for a while. I didn't look demented, but he could see I was in earnest. He said it was not easy for a person to contact one on the earth for the first time and a good medium was essential, if a 'dead' person did not wish to communicate that was the end of it. But if a person loved someone on the earth they would do their utmost to get through. He advised me to write to the College of Psychic Studies, Queensbury Place, South Kensington, London, ask for their literature, and then I could make up my mind. He also advised me to wait three months before contacting Stan to give him more time to adjust. I thanked him for his help and advice. I felt now as if I was getting somewhere.

The following morning I contacted my friend Pat. We had been friends since my family and I returned from South Africa, went to the same church, where her children and mine became friends. Her daughter and Louise were in the church choir. I asked if she would accompany me to London after explaining everything. This she agreed to do. That evening I wrote to the College as suggested by Dr. Israel.

I made one visit and that my last to the crematorium where Stan's name was inscribed in the beautiful book of Remembrance. Relatives can enter a few chosen words. The words I chose were 'God Will Unite Us' - and hoped he would when I made my first visit to a medium. Leaving the crematorium I felt a weight was lifted from me. I also thought I heard a voice saying, "I am not here in this place but with you - don't come back here."

No, I would never return. Although it was kept beautiful, it was still filled with sorrow, one could never get away from it. Stan was with me in spirit. I did not need gravestones or tombstones to remind me of my loved one. One can always have one's own garden of remembrance at home, if one has a garden. I later bought a rose bush, a beautiful pink rose named 'Dearest' - Stan always liked the colour pink. He would like the rose bush to be in our garden not somewhere miles away. Every thought and memory were imprinted on places.

One Door Closes

A sensitive person can easily pick up vibrations whether they be good or bad. A person must leave something of themselves when they die, if only thoughts. These must linger in the air, and good thoughts must of themselves help the bereaved. My thoughts went back to that awful morning. Stan had left for work hurriedly. If only we had known this would happen, I did feel uneasy though but couldn't explain why. The evening before the accident he said, "There are a few papers you should know about, in case anything should happen to me - just write to these people."

"Don't be silly, nothing is going to happen to you," I said.

Did Stan also have a premonition, but didn't like to tell me? In times of illness husbands and wives prepare themselves for the worst. To try and tie up loose ends. Last goodbyes are said and the departed one can then leave in a contented mood (as much as can be expected under the circumstances) - it makes the one left behind a little better to know that they had at least a few words to say to each other. I wasn't with Stan at the last.

His accident was so swift. We didn't have time to say goodbye. In perfect health and mind, keen on his job, he had so much to look forward to, one being our holiday that year. We hoped to visit Spain again. However could I contemplate a holiday again without him. We had never relished separate holidays as many couples seem to enjoy.

Dear God, why didn't the lorry driver die? After all he had caused the accident by cutting right in front of Stan's car. My thoughts grew more hostile - more so when I read in the morning's paper that a man, whom the police were anxiously trying to trace, had killed three women and kidnapped another. My husband had to die whilst this fiend lived and terrorised the public. Friends told me there is a reason for everything - this I disagreed with, and replied where was the justice in a good man being killed whilst a murderer lived. Of course there was no reply. It was not until a long time later - an eternity later - that I learnt there is a reason for everything. Like instant coffee we always demand instant answers to our questions and actions.

Who can understand God's ways, famine, plague, war? There must be an answer to all these if we could only find out. I only knew one thing - a portion of myself had been wrenched away. Peace only came at night to forget the cares of the day. Perhaps I too was in the world of spirit. How glibly the Church speaks of the 'dead' as resting in peace, but how could Stan 'be at peace' if he had tried to contact me? If not he, then whom? As somebody had definitely tried to get through to me. Perhaps peace would only come through an infinite increase of knowledge. To both of us I mean. Until that time I could not be at rest.

Relaxing in the chair that evening, my mind went back to my first encounter with death. My father, Sub-Divisional Inspector at Brixton Police Station, died in the Police Hospital in Godalming, Surrey - only 42 years of age - at three o'clock in the afternoon. My mother and I were present. On arriving home I glanced at the clock and gasped, "Look mother at the clock."

My mother's dazed eyes looked at me, then slowly at our clock on the mantelpiece.

"What about it," she said in a terribly weary voice.

"It has stopped at three o'clock, the exact time Dad died, don't you remember?" I said rather excitedly.

"Well it's only a coincidence," she said in a dull tone.

"But don't you think it odd, especially when that clock never stops, and only Dad winds it up - perhaps he . . ."

"Perhaps he what?"

Mother was looking at me quite strangely by now. I was flustered by now, not knowing what I meant.

"Well, perhaps, even though he is dead perhaps in a way he is trying to reach out. Oh! I don't know, but to me it is much more than coincidence. I am sure there is some good explanation."

My mother stood up.

"Dad is dead, leave it at that, I'll never see him again."

She started to cry. I then stood up.

"I know he is not dead, and I know you will see him again - I just know you will."

My mother looked at me with a flicker of hope in her eyes for one second, then turned away.

After my mother retired that evening I sat thinking. What had made me say she would see my father again? Yet something in my mind which I couldn't put into words convinced me that we would see him.

From an early age, when at Sunday-school, we were taught of the angels of heaven. What was the purpose of it if it were not true?

My second encounter with death was also during the war, when a bomb completely demolished our neighbours home taking half of ours with it. Everyone in our neighbour's home was killed, whilst we lost all our home. The only thing of real value to me was my piano. Whilst searching through the dust and rubble and climbing the half swaying staircase which once led to my bedroom I found a dusty book. I wiped it and opened the pages, and to my surprise found photos of spirit people. I was so fascinated I sat down amidst the dust and started to read. It seemed a bit weird. I never knew my father owned such a book. He was a Mason and possessed a beautiful bible, which I was never allowed to open. It had gold leafed pages. I think the Masons have some affiliation with Spiritualists, they do not disagree at any rate as the orthodox churches do. Our neighbours on the other side escaped, of which I was thankful, as we were very friendly with them, and I was great friends with their son Ernie who used to take me rowing in the park in the summer.

The third death (of my special friend Ivor) was more than I could bear. He was in the Fleet Air Arm, and died one year after my father. He was shot down. It was then that I joined the Auxiliary Territorial Service. After the initial training I was posted to a camp opposite Hyde Park. The guns were deafening, and one girl couldn't take the noise and bombing so was replaced. It was here that I think divine intervention acted. There was a vacant bed in my room which was taken by a new girl who had come to replace the one who left. Within a few minutes of introducing ourselves we discovered not only had we lived in the same town, but had attended the same school. Even to the fact that both our fathers' had died within a few years of each other. This was really a coincidence.

At the end of the day we sat and I told her of my father's accident, and how my mother couldn't speak about it. Also about the book of spirit photographs. I was surprised when she said, "Of course I know my father isn't really dead."

"I've always thought that too," I said, thinking of the stopped clock, and mentioning it. She nodded in agreement. I certainly wasn't prepared for what she next said, which was so casual.

"Yes, but my father came and sat next to me on my bed."

I felt embarrassed and must have looked it. Hope he doesn't come tonight I thought.

"Have you told your mother?" I said cautiously.

"No, she wouldn't understand."

"She may do one day - she isn't ready for it yet."

"When he sat on your bed, was he . . ." I stopped unable to get the words out.

"He wasn't naked if that's what you mean," she said.

It's exactly what I meant. She was quick to interpret.

"No he was just wearing his old suit."

"Couldn't he have worn his new suit?"

A naive question no doubt. She gave me a quick look. Was I pulling her leg.

"I can see you know nothing about Spiritualism," she said, starting to explain.

"When a spirit (we don't call them ghosts) passes into the next dimension they take their brain, memory, identity and personality with them. They can come back to those they love, if and when the time is right. There must be enough power in a room. It is similar to a medium in a seance, she must have enough power to enable the spirit or spirits to get through to her so she can pass on any message to the person concerned in the room but when . . . Are you interested?" she said.

"Yes, sounds a bit involved," I said carefully.

"It is, and people don't know how much time and trouble they take to get through to us. When I mentioned his old suit, he was happy in it, they still retain their memory as I said."

This really was the strangest conversation I had ever had. I mentioned the spirit photographs I had found after the bombing. Then I asked her why her father hadn't appeared to her mother. "Perhaps I loved him more than she did - they only come to those they love or who love them - or maybe he knows it will scare her, and they wouldn't do that."

I told her about my boy-friend's death.

"He will come back to you when the time is right, or when you get the right medium, that is most important. You have to be on the same

45

wavelength as the medium. Your father will also try to come back.
It does help a lot if they believed in this before they passed over."
It was a most interesting conversation, and one that stands out in my
memory. A week later she too had been posted. I was later posted to
Edinburgh. I never saw her again.
And it was here I met Vivienne. These then were my first encounters
with death.

Chapter Seven

HOPE

We count the hours these dreams of ours, false and hollow.
Do we go hence and find they are not dead?
Joys, we dimly apprehend, faces that smiled and fled
hopes born here, and born to end, shall we follow?

A Question by Matthew Arnold.

Correspondence was awaiting me on the mat the following morning from the College of Psychic Studies. Dr Israel had advised me to wait three months, but I couldn't wait that long to find out whether Stan was alive or dead - perhaps desperately wanting to contact me.

I made a pot of tea and carefully read all the leaflets. They had many things going on at the College. After breakfast I sat down and wrote to the College, making my first appointment with a medium. I chose the 5th June, which was my wedding anniversary.

So exactly four months after Stan's accident I arrived at the College. Pat had kept her word and accompanied me. I was glad of her company as I felt a trifle nervous. I had never been to such a place before. It was not that I was frightened of contacting Stan, but was a little apprehensive, more I think that I may break down at his first message, if ever I received one that is. I tried to think that it was like a telephone wire with the medium acting as operator, which they are really. I was told not to expect much at the first sitting.

After waiting about ten minutes I was shown into a small room. I was shaking, feeling very nervous. My medium was a Mrs Doris Collins. I liked the look of her immediately. She looked like a really sympathetic person. She sensed I was tense, and told me just to relax. There was a small table between us. She said a small prayer, and was

47

quiet for a while. I had taken a book and pencil just in case a few words came through. The first words did come through and I nearly fell off my chair.

"Your husband is here and he says his name is Stanley - no Stan, that is what you called him," she said brightly.

"At last you have come," he is saying.

"He is in the spirit world."

"Oh!" I said.

"Do you know what I'm talking about?" she said.

"Well he's dead, isn't he? I said, not knowing what to say.

She shook her head a trifle sadly.

"Well you might think he's dead, but he's very much alive, and he is putting his arms around you and gives you some roses."

I looked around, but of course I couldn't see him as I am not gifted like she and not a clairvoyant.

"He is also saying that his watch and his photo are in your handbag." I gasped at this.

"Can I see them please." She held the watch.

"He remembers the dress you are wearing - a wedding." (I was wearing the dress I wore at my daughter's wedding). Then all the names of aunts and uncles were mentioned who had died. But the thing which really convinced me (if ever I was in doubt that is) was when Doris Collins said, "Your husband is saying we have just missed our wedding anniversary."

She was holding Stan's watch and said, "What a clever man, he is saying when he passed over his mother received him, but he said he wanted to go back to Joyce." At this point I cried.

"He is saying do not cry - it had to be. It was an awful shock to him as he didn't realise he was dead until he came back to you and spoke to you in your home, but received no reply! He is saying something about money. 'It wasn't my fault,' and 'You must get the compensation.' Do you know what that means?"

I quickly explained about his accident. She nodded, and continued. "He is saying the lorry hit him side on - he saw your face and nothing more. You were the love of his life."

"He was the love of mine," I whispered.

Mrs Collins continued, "He is saying, 'I'll walk beside you'"- from a favourite piece of music. "He will also be with you and you will never be separated. You are twin-souls. He is also saying give my love to the boys and girls. He is gone. That was wonderful," said Mrs Collins, "considering it was the first time he has communicated."

I was so overjoyed and excited that I hugged her. This was without any doubt the most wonderful day of my life. She was as pleased as I was. She had put concentration and all her energy into that sitting. She said that he was becoming tired at the end, but had made a wonderful effort. I said I would like to return in three months time. I returned to the waiting room and met Pat.

"You look transformed," she said.

"Let us go and find somewhere to have tea," I said, "I have so much to tell you." I felt six feet high. Over a pot of tea and some scones I related everything. Pat just couldn't believe it. I read out the message from my short-hand notebook. After, she said that she often thought her 'dead' relations were with her. She would never have mentioned this if I hadn't opened the subject.

A new chapter had suddenly unfolded for me. I could not go back now.

Chapter Eight

A WARNING

They err who tell us love can die,
With life all other passions fly,
All others are but vanity,
In heaven ambition cannot dwell
Nor avarice in the vaults of hell;
Earthly passions of the earth
They perish where they have their birth
But love is indestructible
It's holy flame forever burneth
From heaven it came-
To heaven it returneth,
Too oft on earth a troubled guest
At times deceived, at times oppressed,
It here is tried and purified,
Then hath in heaven it's perfect rest;
It soweth here with toil and care-
But the harvest time of love is there.

By Southey.

From desperation to anticipation - now acclamation, I now knew beyond any doubt that as the above poem so poignantly tells, love cannot die with death. Recalling the message Doris Collins relayed to me, even the inflections in her voice were the way Stan would have spoken. Words cannot express the joy I felt. Even if people should not believe, I believed, and Stan was only speaking to me, although he named all the children in turn.

I knew the Vicar and people at the church were sure to be interested, and delighted that at last life had now some meaning for me. Hadn't I already told the vicar after Stan's funeral that I knew I would see him again, perhaps hoping desperately for assurance. The reply was, "If you believe that then it's alright." But the tone lacked conviction. This was no belief but a proven fact in my case surely.

I wrote to Vivienne. Here was one person who would really be interested, as she was still in a state of shock and needed comfort. I gave her the name of a Spiritualist Church near her which I found in the 'Psychic News,' telling her to go to their demonstrations of clairvoyance. A week later I had a reply. She hadn't been at all well but would go as soon as she was able. She was very interested in my message. I had bought a large beautiful white leather book in which I would write each message and the date I received it. After my message that day Doris Collins told me to buy the book 'The University of Spiritualism' by Harry Boddington, or borrow it from the College library, which I did. She also told me to visit the Spiritualist Church in my area. I didn't know where it was, and didn't know we had one in our town, as it wasn't advertised.

My mind went back to the awful night of the accident. I remembered so plainly saying to Stan, "Don't leave me." So God had answered my prayer. I had also prayed for Stan the day of the funeral, for surely he must be in a state of shock. This was confirmed by Doris when she said, "It was an awful shock to him." This will come as a shock to many I believe, who think the departed are really dead with no feelings or memory left. We have the churches to thank for this appalling lack of knowledge, which they could know if they would take the trouble to find out. In the first Christian Churches mediums did take the services and healing took place, soon taken over by the priests who condemned all mediums and thousands were killed all over Europe. One of the biggest disgraces in our history.

We had never discussed death except for one evening a few weeks before his accident. Stan suddenly said, "If I am involved in an accident I want to go straight out. I couldn't bear to be crippled." So God had answered his prayer too. The subject was too painful. It was the awful thought of separation. To be a separate entity again was unthinkable. At least one friend called each day, and showed surprise and disbelief. Nothing like this had ever happened to them. Perhaps the medium could read my mind they said. But how can a mind be read, it is not a physical thing. It directs the brain. I realised later they were trying to put me off because *they* didn't believe, therefore it must be wrong. I forget the number of times I was told that the Old Testament said quite plainly that one shouldn't contact the dead and that a witch should be be burnt. (The Church literally did this much to their shame). I told them Doris Collins wasn't a witch - she had in fact been the only person who had helped me. Also, I was quick to point out that Stan had contacted her not the other way round. I also mentioned that in the New Testament, a good thousand years after the Old Testament, Jesus, before his death, promised his disciples that he would send a comforter. As the world knows, according to the Bible he came back and spoke to them. I thought Christianity was based upon this event, that this was the essence of Christianity that we will live again, but no one commented upon this. It seemed it was all beyond them. It made them think and they weren't used to that. As for me my life had now changed. Knowing that as each day sped by it would bring me nearer Stan, made life more bearable. There was now a purpose to life, and so much to learn. But there were still the endless nights, and our favourite records which I played often still upset me.

I realised it would take a long time, and that it would have to be in my time.

I cannot recall exactly when I started to notice odd behaviour in friends and acquaintances. Was it my imagination? I would see a person whom I knew walk towards me on the same side of the road, look up, see me, then dart across the road to the other side. I would call after them, but no greeting, just a half-hearted wave. People from the church would bump into me, promise to call, but never did. So much for their Christian upbringing - their promises were lightly given. When I do make a promise I do my utmost to keep it.

The thing I looked forward to most was the mail. Vivienne wrote once a month, long letters, but as her writing was so small, it was difficult to decipher. She was finding it difficult to adjust also. One morning I found two letters on the mat. I eagerly opened one then gave a gasp, and an all consuming anger swept over me. The letter, from a member of the Church, informed me that the vicar's wife had journeyed to London and had seen Dr. Israel, telling him he should not see me. I was outraged and wrote and told her so. It was only in my best interest I was told. She had forgotten it was by the courtesy of the Churches Fellowship for Psychic and Spiritual Studies that he had given the lecture in the first place.

Furious, I opened the second letter. A pious note from another 'Christian' telling me not to meddle in things of a supernatural nature. It could affect my health. She would pray for me. This was too much. I strode around the room swearing and shouting, letting out all the pent up emotions of the past months. Why can people not realise that we all act differently in bereavement, and we also have a right to do so without interference. I did not believe what the Church taught and wanted to find out for myself, so I was the odd one out.

The following morning there was a knock on the door. Opening it I saw it was my neighbour, a Roman Catholic. He tried to push his way in. How he ever found out that I had been to the College I do not know.

"It's not really your husband who came through," he said.

"How would you know?" I said rudely. "How could the medium have known all about Stan's accident, if not from him?"

"The Devil told him to tell her."

I lost my self-control and told him to go to hell - perhaps he'd find the Devil there and could join him.

This upset me for the remainder of the week. I couldn't help thinking how narrow-minded Christians were. Thinking their religion and their's alone held all the answers. Apart from that, it seemed I was not entitled to an opinion of my own. I was also ostracised for telling the truth when asked, would I give up Spiritualism? No, never - not for anyone or anything.

People go to extraordinary lengths telling you what you must or must not do. So when I saw a middle-aged couple walking up the path holding a book, I prepared myself for another outburst. When they knocked at the door, I was surprised to find the lady was a teacher in the Church of England Sunday school, and I had seen her in church many times. They said they were sorry to hear of Stan's accident, but they were Spiritualists even though they attended the local church.

The vicar did not know and she never told him, because she would have been dismissed. She handed me the book saying I could borrow it, but she would like it back. When I opened it I saw it was the same book I had found in my house, of spirit photographs. She told me the name of the person who ran the Spiritualist Church in Maidstone, and they would take me along if I wished to go.

These were the first kind words I had heard since I had first decided to investigate Spiritualism, by reading books etc. I told them I had read 'On The Edge Of The Etheric' by Arthur Findlay. They nodded - a wonderful book - for everybody who wanted to find out how the two worlds meet.

I cannot thank them enough. The following Sunday I joined them. It was a small modern church, clean and bright, with flowers. The President, Mrs Dorothy White was a small neat lady nicely dressed. She had worked hard for this church - and practically ran it single handed. The medium that day would be a Mrs Florence Sporton, and she was very good I was told. The service opened with a hymn, then a prayer. Then it was time for the demonstration of clairvoyance. She came immediately to me. A tall smart looking lady - very direct. She said I had been through a terrible time, but my husband was sending his love. He wanted me to go out and buy a pink candle.

"It must be pink," she repeated. "Light it at night before you go to bed and you will see something."

That was the end of my message. I thanked her. She then went to another. They were mostly middle-aged people, but one young lad about nineteen years of age was sitting in the front.

The medium told him he was going out with a young girl at the moment, but she was definitely not the girl for him and he would meet the right one in about two years time. We all looked at him, he just nodded as though he agreed with her. Folk may say she hadn't the right telling him who or who not to see, but maybe his mother in the spirit world or some relation could see. He could still have continued seeing his present girl friend, even marrying her, but if she was not the right one, the marriage would end in divorce. Happy marriages are made in heaven. Everyone on this earth I am sure has a twin-soul, if we wait long enough they will turn up. I don't think it is necessary to visit a marriage bureau. One may be living the other side of the earth, but if it is meant to happen, it will happen. Stan for example was living in India when a child, when they returned to England his mother died. Through his father marrying my mother (arranged by spirit I am sure) this brought us together.

The following day I remembered what Mrs Sporton had said about the pink candle, and had to visit half a dozen shops before I found a large one.

"Does it have to be pink," said one assistant after having looked through a few boxes, "I have plenty of red ones here."

I thanked her but said it had to be pink. She shrugged. I found one and later that evening lit it, and waited. Nothing happened. I did this each evening for about a week, still nothing happened. At the end of the week I lit it again, waited, and thought I saw a faint glow. With mounting excitement the glow grew larger all around the candle and then all the colours of the rainbow appeared like a halo. It was beautiful. I hardly dared breathe. I couldn't believe my eyes. I called Louise so she could see it also. I called several times and she came running into my room. I told her, and looked again at the candle, but the colours gradually faded away. I don't think she believed me. It was for my eyes alone. All she could see was an ordinary candle burning in the usual way. I wished that those in the spirit world could have just held the colours a little while longer so Louise could have seen it.

I went to the Spiritualist church every week after that, and the following week mentioned the incident. Others had seen psychic phenomena of different types. One lady had seen her husband quite clearly standing on the lawn in her back garden. For a few moments only. Another lady had taken a photo of her favourite rose tree. It was where her son used to sit before he was killed on his motorbike. When the film was developed a statue of an angel with large wings could clearly be seen by the rose tree. She handed it around so all could see. This person was very psychic and had the gift of psychic photography. Many people do have this gift without realising it. Some may see a huge white blur on a negative and think it is a fault in the processing, but keep on trying. Faces sometimes appear of relations who have passed over. The College of Psychic Studies have books and pictures of this subject. That afternoon there was a new medium. The message that day was short and to the point.

"Keep on the path - don't go backwards. A man is holding a red rose out to you. There is so much love coming from this man. He is saying thankyou for the flowers, he says there were five in a vase."

I walked out of the church as though I was on air. How lovely to have a message like that. The thankyou was for the five anemones I had on my dressing table. There had been red roses in my wedding bouquet. It was a miracle to me that we could communicate. The mediums were never paid for their services (unlike priests) - the gift they had was worth more than gold. If our Anglican Church had only employed the services of a medium I would never have left it. The dwindling congregations in our churches now are proof that people want comfort, something they cannot get in their church.

I would say by now I was a devout Spiritualist, but still found it difficult to break away entirely from the church I had found happiness in since returning from South Africa. So one Sunday found me at the Communion Service. All seemed to be going well, and I joined others by the communion rail. I noticed there was a new vicar who had replaced the old one temporarily whilst he was on holiday. The verger was handing out the bread, and the new vicar holding the wine out to each person at the rail. When he came to me, to my surprise he said, "Do you believe in God?"

I had never known a vicar to speak during the Communion offertory. "Yes," I replied, just managing to stop myself saying the words 'Do you?' "

"Do you renounce the Devil," he said.

I was completely taken aback at this.

"Yes," I again replied, not knowing who the devil was, also what the devil he was getting at.

"Will you renounce Spiritualism?" he asked in a louder voice.

"No I won't," I replied in an even louder tone.

It was his turn to be taken aback. He stepped backwards nearly bumping into the communion table containing the bread and wine. Someone tittered. He recovered himself and was passing by holding the cup to the next person.

"Aren't you even going to give me a blessing?" I said dryly.

He paused, then came back and reluctantly handed me the bread and wine. So, someone must have told him - who I wondered. I had not met him before this. It must have been the verger. He only lived a few doors from me.

This pathetic human being who called himself a vicar (luckily not of our parish) was responsible for the spiritual welfare of the community. I noticed for the first time that healing was introduced, and both he and a sideswoman did the healing. After the healing, and after the service I approached him and asked if he would like to come to my church and see how they did healing.

"I'm not coming to your church," he shouted, "it's full of evil spirits."

I nearly smacked his face.

"How dare you say such things about my church." I said.

He saw I was angry and started to move away.

"How can healing be other than good - wherever it is practised?"

"It's the Devil who is doing the healing," the pathetic figure replied.

"You want to read the New Testament sometime. Jesus practised healing and told his disciples to do it also, actually telling them to go and do likewise."

It seemed incredible I had to actually explain the Gospel to him.

"If what we are doing is wrong, then what Jesus did was also wrong." Healing should be done in all hospitals, churches, all places of sickness and for animals in distress. I also told him that in my church people could also bring in their sick animals. Can you see an Anglican Church allowing this? This discussion had taken place outside the church. Talking to Pat a few weeks later I learned that the vicar's wife had mentioned that I shouldn't be allowed back into the church. I was speechless. Together with others I had helped to dust and polish the pews, arranged flowers and distributed magazines for about ten years. Well! If that was Christianity they could keep it.

I wanted to buy a flowering cherry tree for Stan and hoped it would be placed in the churchyard. This was mentioned to a member of the Church Council. A few weeks went by but nothing was mentioned to me. It would have meant a lot to me. I felt by then as if I really was an outsider. How can an intelligent person continue to visit these 'Black Holes' - I left the church which I had attended along with my family for so long. It was a beautiful little village church, but it was now time to move on. I never went back. I suddenly felt free.

I think the narrowness of the Christian Church (in no way due to the founder) finally came home to me, when one day I turned on the radio and a service was about to start. The opening words were, "Let us give thanks and blessings to all Christians everywhere."

No mention of the millions of Jews, Buddhists, Muslims, and the thousands of other religions in the world. This is where Spiritualism is greater, as it embraces people from all walks of life and religions. Anyone can come into our churches. A muslim family came into our church for healing. Would they have entered a Christian Church - or what is more to the point, would they have been welcomed?

Chapter Nine

HOW I OVERCAME GRIEF

Even so in Christ shall all be made alive.

Corinthians Ch. 15. v 22.

I made a new friend at the Spiritualist Church in Maidstone. Her name was Anne, she too was recently widowed, but for her it was more harrowing , as arriving home one day she found her husband hanging in the shed. I do apologise to her for writing this, but I know she too would like others to know that by whatever means they die they too can come back, so I hope this will bring comfort to all those whose loved ones have committed suicide. We all meet up again with those we love, and it is only love which is the motive for bringing them back, whatever the Church says. I hope readers will use their common sense.

Anne and I became quite friendly, and had quite a few things in common. My brother had been to the same Masonic School as her son in Hertfordshire. Only the sons of masons were admitted.

I was also surprised to find that another lady whose children attended the same school as mine was also interested in Spiritualism, especially as she attended the Anglican Church - my old church. Her father-in-law was the President of a Spiritualist Church. We also had much in common, as her husband held a senior post in the police, my father having been in the police. Her name was Betty, we also became friends.

It so happened that Anne, Betty and I were invited to join a circle at the home of Mrs Dorothy White (the President of the Spiritualist Church) every fortnight. Mrs Florence Sporton would give private messages, and would also teach a little philosophy, and how to tune into spirit, she would also read passages from 'In Tune with the Infinite' by Waldo Trine. A book which will appeal to all ages and tastes. It contains some beautiful passages.

It was a small gathering, about twelve. I looked forward to these fortnightly meetings. Meeting others who also had a death in the family, and hearing how they coped. They all said it was only the knowledge of life after death which kept them going. I did not miss my old church or my friends, as I felt they were on another plane to me. I could not even speak to them about my interests, there was a host of things to discover. If my old church was dead, Spiritualism was very much alive.

The composer Mendelssohn once said, "Feed the senses with the beauty and purity of true harmony. Much that is of evil can also be gathered from sound: one can only vibrate to those chords which are within one."

Friday evening was the evening when I played my records. The children were always out then. Only two years before Stan's accident he bought a record which to us captured the mood of Spain where we spent our annual holiday. It was the 'Iberia Suite' by Albeniz, also 'Goyescas Intermezzo' by Granados. He loved Spain, their music and the people. Music lifted me spiritually as nothing else could. Far better than a church service, and I hoped that one day I would have the pleasure of meeting those great masters, Brahms, Beethoven, and the great Russian composers. People who have never listened to a concert at the Albert Hall have missed one of the great joys in life. Music played an important part in overcoming grief. And yet some said I was becoming too morbid - should get out more. I found people more and more irritating, forever telling me what they think I ought to do. Music to me was not only therapeutic - it was a life-saver. Wasn't Stan also listening? They weren't deaf just because they were in the world of spirit.

One medium told me the spirit world was so close it was unbelievable. One could either shut them out or include them, like you would your own family at home. Music will draw them in time of jollification. Mendelssohn also said, "Man has now learnt to catch vibrations, to imprison sound and carry it whither he wills. Does it not make him pause to think how much he still misses, what vast stores of sound still remain? Vibrations of the past, of the future! How vast a science. Man is only at the beginning. Here in spirit it is understood, and the vibrations are used by us in such manner as is not yet understood by earth. Many believe that it is only by waves of thought that we communicate in spirit, they forget the glory of sound that is ours, and how much the beauty and perfection of true harmony enters into spirit life. The blending of the voices, the colours responding to the sounds. Does it not call up a mental picture of beauty, which all may see when earth has taught it's lesson. Train your spirit upwards by sound, perfect and good - not downwards. Both are possible!!"

These beautiful thoughts were received from the spirit world by a medium in trance, and were compiled into a book (given to me by a friend after Stan's accident) called 'The Fellowship Of The Golden Triangle.' I read a little each morning.

Facing a new day can be an awesome and very formidable, even frightening experience for many people. Those who have no friends, who are cut off from the outside world. Those who's work bores them. Those who by their very nature drive others away. Those who feel inadequate and insecure. Those who seek a change of job, but feel too timid to make an adjustment. Some of us at some time may have fitted into one of these categories. What then can be more comforting than a few uplifting words from the spirit world where they really care. We are told we only have to ask in real sincerity for help and it shall be given.

The best things in life it seems are still free. True love, and true friendships, so I was always pleased to receive letters from Vivienne. She still wrote each month - not one page - but about ten. She, like me, still found it difficult to adjust to life without one's husband. I sometimes took the Intercity to Birmingham and encouraged her to visit her local Spiritualist Church. I passed on psychic books and any message I thought would interest her. One did very much.

It so happened that I heard about a weekend course given at the Arthur Findlay College later in the year and asked Vivienne if she would care to accompany me. A well known medium gave addresses in trance. Bookings could be taken immediately. Vivienne said she would like to, but would like to think it over before booking. She couldn't attend if she wasn't well, but if she couldn't go perhaps I could go as she would like to know any message I received, if I should be lucky enough to receive one that is. I did mention in one of my letters that Spiritualism had saved my life and sanity, and was very surprised when she replied saying why don't I write a book. I replied immediately saying I wouldn't know where to start, and anyway I didn't know enough about the subject, but her letter made me think. There were many courses I wished to attend, and many more books to be read. I would have to type it and that would take a long time. Perhaps I would in a few years.

I continued to attend the home circle in Dorothy's home each fortnight. All from different walks of life but drawn by our common interest. We sometimes attended the College of Music where we listened to music and lectures in philosophy.

Every three months I attended the College of Psychic Studies and bought a book, attending a lecture in the evening, but solely for a sitting with Doris Collins. Each time Stan came through.

The second message I received Doris said, "Your husband is remembering the wonderful time you both had in Amsterdam, and the paintings of Van Gogh. He says, 'You always spoiled me. We had a wonderful life. I never thought it would be like this in spirit. You contacted me through the Churches Fellowship. The lorry hit me side-on. I did not die immediately. Keep my memory alive with colour. Always have flowers in front of the mirror. I am trying to help your friend.'" (A friend of mine suffered from depression).

"'Get the compensation, I have always looked after you. I love you.'" Doris then laughed as she said, "Your husband is saying that damned side fence has fallen down again."

I also laughed at that, but then immediately felt sad that I couldn't see him, but realised at once how lucky I was that I could get a message from him. How many widows in the world would have been glad to have received such a message?

"The side lamp needs mending." Doris was talking again.

"It is very difficult for them to communicate the first few times. Things are hazy, they cannot sometimes remember people's first names, let alone surnames. He is asking if you want to ask him any questions?"

I thought quickly. There were so many I didn't know how to begin,

as I hadn't been prepared for this. If only I had known I would have written them down. I said the first thing that came into my mind.
"Will you wait for me?"
"Of course."
"Have you been home at all?"
"Of course, it's my home. Don't you remember when the lights went off and on on Guy Fawkes night? That was me. I get help from people here. I never thought it would be like this. I am with my mother. She helped me over. You have a broader outlook on life. I am contacting you through a reflectograph. Love draws us. There is no going back. My watch is for you, it brings me nearer to you. I have my own garden and equipment. You have come to me several times. If Auntie Lily asks tell her.(My aunt Lily's husband John passed away a few years before Stan, and she never got over his passing).

Give my love to my father (which I did, and he accepted it quite naturally, much to my surprise!) I do wish the boys could believe in this, but don't worry. This helps you by contacting me. My firm has been good to you. (This was true as the firm gave me £8000). My case has not come up yet. The lorry had no brakes the day of my accident, it banged into my car.

I put my hand out to save the folder with all my papers, but it was too late. Your church does not approve of you contacting me, but tell them you are speaking to your husband NOT the devil. I am alive and with God. There is a power which generates. I feel it all around and know it's there. I still work with people and my mother is with me. We brought our children up in a Christian way. Louise is restless and wishes to go abroad. Let them go dear. The house is paid for. I'll be with you all at Christmas. My present to you is a small cross on a chain. (Louise did buy me one). So much I would like to tell you. I love you. We've had so many happy years together. Say hello to the boys and love to the girls. I am strengthening you through the auric field. I don't want you to go to work. You have enough to do."

This was really a wonderful message, and I wrote it down quickly, and then wrote it in my leather-bound book when I reached home. I know I could never have survived without these messages. And to think the Church would ban this comfort from it's congregations. If only they knew the harm they were doing.

There were many times of course when I became upset. The evenings were the worst when I saw all the husbands arriving home from work. One young man regularly passed my house at the same time each day. It always coincided with one of the boys returning home from work. Then one day I realised I hadn't seen him for a long time. I made enquiries and was told he had died. His young wife lived on the estate a few roads away. I sat down and wondered what I should do. I had the knowledge, but how to put it into practice. Would she listen to me? Would it be an intrusion into her private life? Then I went back over the last year, and realised I would have given anything to have been told what I now know. I made up my mind. It was June, my wedding anniversary, and my sweet peas were out. I picked a large bunch, and with a book about Spiritualism I very hesitantly knocked at her door. I felt like running away when I heard footsteps. If I was quick I could run up the path and round the corner, but I thought this would be a cowards way out. The door was opened and a young woman stared at me.

"I've brought these for you," I said. "I heard about your husband and I am so sorry."

"Did you know him?" she asked in surprise.

"No, but I always used to see him in the morning, and at night on his way home. I have brought you a book which you may like to read." She looked at it, then invited me in. I explained about Stan's accident. She listened sympathetically. Then I mentioned the book I had read which led me to attend the College of Psychic Studies in London, how I had contacted the Churches Fellowship of Psychic and Spiritual Studies and the trouble I had experienced with the church in the village. She nodded at this. She seemed interested, especially when I mentioned the Spiritualist church in the town. After half an hour I thought I had better leave. It was whilst she was showing me out that she broke down for the first time. They had only been married a few years. She was a nurse, and had seen a few deaths, but still could not cope with the death of one so dear to her. I said she could help him by doing her work as well as she could, and they would be re-united. She was impressed by the messages I received. I said good bye and told her I would keep in touch.

After I arrived home I hoped I had done the right thing, and had not upset her. She did break down but by crying it had eased her, she had to get it out of her system, and that was the natural way. At least she knew there was one neighbour who cared and had suffered a bereavement like hers.

I didn't see her until a month later when I was shopping. She was with her mother and looked much better.

Chapter Ten

THE EFFECTUAL POWER OF PRAYER

Has anyone turned to Him in vain,
sought rest, comfort and found no answer.
Indeed one cannot send out an appeal in
all sincerity and go empty away.

Anon.

It was now summer, June 1975, a whole year after Stan's accident.
What a year, I could never go through that again. I thanked God for
the friends I had in the Spiritualist Church and my mother who came
when she could. I was also glad that Angela had decided to marry
Richard in the November before Stan's death, so he was able to give
her away, although at the time I would have liked a summer wedding.
Strange how things seem to fall into place.

It was also strawberry time, and I suggested to the family that we pick
some strawberries from a nearby farm and take some to my mother.
We took about ten pounds. I knew she would make jam. It was a
Saturday and Roger drove Louise and I. Anthony was working. Once
again we had to pass the spot where Stan's accident had occured.
Nobody spoke. It didn't matter now. I knew we would never be
separated.

Mother had prepared a lovely tea. Afterwards we went for a walk, but
on the way back home mother slipped. Roger had to run back and
fetch the car. On arriving home she said that she was alright, but we
contacted her sister Eva (who lived a mile away) who came to stay
with her. By that time it was eight o'clock and we had a good hour's
drive home, so we left. Aunt Eva said she would keep in touch.

The following Tuesday I was having a private sitting in the church with Florrie. It was two o'clock.

"Your husband is here, he is very agitated - keeps on saying water, water. Do you know what that means?" she said quickly.

"Well there is the River Medway at the end of our road," I replied, feeling startled, wondering if anything had happened to one of the family.

"No, I think it is someone's name, do you know anyone by the name of Walter?"

She was insistant it was a name. It then clicked into place.

"Stan's father was named Walter, but we never called him that," I said. (His father had never been in the best of health, so I wasn't surprised if he should go suddenly).

"Yes, that's right, he says he has to go to Walter, he is on an errand of mercy, he cannot stay. I'm sorry there is no more from him today."

My messages were always longer than that. I left the church quickly and went home. So poor grandad was going, oh well, it had to come.

The telephone was ringing as I entered the hall. I answered it to hear aunt Eva saying, "Joyce I have some bad news for you."

"Yes, I think I know, is it about Walter?" I said quickly. I felt an uneasy silence.

"No Joyce, it is about your mother - she is dead Joyce."

I heard my aunt crying at the other end of the phone. I couldn't answer.

"Joyce, did you hear what I said?" my aunt repeated.

"Yes," I replied dully, "I knew something dreadful was happening when I went to the church today."

I then repeated the message given to me. My God what a shock it was. I sank down on the stairs whilst aunt Eva related her side of the story. After I had visited her that evening, after mother's fall, aunt Eva and uncle Bill had insisted on taking mother to hospital the next day. No bones were broken. Mother was allowed home the following day, the 1st July. Mother felt well enough to go shopping, but on returning home felt unwell and stopped at her neighbour's house. She was taken home, but collapsed. The neighbour phoned an ambulance, and after being admitted to hospital mother passed away. The time was 1.30pm on 1st July and at 2 o'clock that very day I received a message from Stan at the Spiritualist church about Walter (his

70

Father). So Stan had known before I did, and was preparing me for the shock which I was about to receive. He didn't tell me it was my mother who had died because he knew it would be too much of a shock. It was best I receive it from my aunt. They were preparing me for bad news.

"Dear God, first Stan now mother - who would be next?" I said to myself, as things always happened in threes, one of the laws in the universe I was once told, which made sense at the time. I was still sitting by the phone when Anthony arrived home from work. He was speechless, as mother had last visited us only a few weeks before. The rest of the family arrived and it was a subdued meal we ate. They were fond of mother, although she could be strict.

When the family were in bed I sat in the chair going over events. Mother had been a great help when Stan had gone. How was I going to cope. I would miss her coming to visit, and who would look after Stan's father now? He had barely got over Stan's death. I didn't know how I was going to get over this second tragedy. At least Stan wouldn't be so lonely now I thought.

The following day I was in a terrible state and felt suffocated, but had to go to mother's bungalow where I met a tearful aunt Eva. She had agreed to notify all the relations, but I said I should first contact my brother Victor who was in Canada, as he would naturally wish to come to the funeral. He would have to book a flight, and should be notified immediately. My aunt and I had to discuss refreshments for the family and her friends. After all the arrangements had been made I left for home. It had been a long day. A three hour journey both ways left me tired, and I was still in shock. I was glad to arrive home.

I was so glad we had taken the strawberries to her that day. An inner voice prompted me to visit her. If I hadn't obeyed that voice I would never have seen her. It was undoubtedly Stan trying to get through to me.

The day I dreaded at last arrived. It was a beautiful sunny morning. My brother Victor had arrived the day before the funeral from Vancouver looking distraught and tired from his long journey. He was terribly upset as we all were. Mother had written a letter to him every week of his life from his earliest days when at boarding school, throughout the army in Cyprus, and when in Hong Kong working at

71

a hospital in a rehabilitation centre for refugees. Then finally in Canada where he worked for another hospital. He would miss her letters. He was very young when my father died, and remembered little of him. He also couldn't bring himself to believe the messages I related to him. He had studied psychology and many other 'oligies,' and I naturally thought he would have been interested in psychic matters, especially when they were a proven fact. Perhaps when he received a personal message from my mother he would be fully convinced. People demand proof and rightly so.

I had been in mother's bedroom, thinking I would have to sort out her clothes the coming week, when there was a light tap on the door.

"The funeral cars have arrived," my aunt said quietly.

The shocked relations stood around the grave where my father and now my mother lay buried, still unable to believe she had gone. We had only spoken to her a few days before. All this due to a fall whilst on a walk. I thought I heard Stan say, "Don't give way, be strong." After the funeral we returned to my mother's house where aunt Eva and I served light refreshments to relations I had not seen for many years. We naturally assumed it would be a peaceful meal, so were not prepared for the commotion which followed, when one aunt said her husband had had more wreaths on his grave than my mother! My brother just exploded at this. This aunt always said things to upset the family. This resulted in half the aunts leaving. Who was it who said one can choose ones friends but not ones relations? I just couldn't be bothered with family quarrels. I thought my aunt would have least had a bit more tact.

The following day I phoned Peggy, Victor's mother-in-law. Peggy had been very good friends with my mother and had also felt a suffocating presence in her house. It was she who I had phoned on hearing of mother's death. Peggy was very psychic, and once when her mother was very ill, she was sitting by her bed when two old ladies dressed in black Edwardian dresses suddenly appeared to her. They told her to sit all night by her mother's bed bathing her head at intervals throughout the night. By early morning she had fully recovered.

Peggy said I was the only member of the family she could talk to on these matters. Nobody would have believed her. The following morning when the doctor called, he was so astonished to see the patient sitting up in bed smiling that he nearly died of shock. He fully expected to find her dead.

From the day of my mother's funeral Stan's father couldn't look after himself, so Stan's younger brother arranged for him to live at his house. But the shock of Stan's death and now my mother's was too much for him and within three weeks he too was dead.

It was a warm day in July. The children didn't come this time. I journeyed by train to my aunt's house. From there we made the same journey to the same cemetary. Stan now had both his mother and father with him and my mother too. It was I who would be lonely. It had been a beautiful day. I thought if Stan and our parents had all been alive we could have spent a lovely time on the beach.

I arrived home three hours later feeling very jaded and worn out. I had seen enough of cemeteries.

It had been a beautiful day when my father had died, and to many mourners (who know nothing of the world of spirit) it can be more painful for them as they think the departed one will never again see the sun and flowers.

THE BLESSED DEAD

Oh! it is sweet to think - of those that are departed;
While murmured Aves sink - to silence tenderhearted;
While tears that have no pain - Are tranquilly distilling;
And the dead live again - in hearts that love is filling.

Yet not as in the days - of earthly ties we love them;
For they are touched with rays - from light that is above them;
Another sweetness shines - around their wellknown features;
God with His glory shines - His dearly-ransomed creatures.

Ah! they are more our own - since now they are God's only;
And each one that has gone - has left our heart less lonely;
He mourns not seasons fled - who now in Him possesses;
Treasures of many dead - in their dear Lord's caresses.

One Door Closes

Dear dead! they have become - like guardian angels to us;
And distant heaven like home - through them begins to woo us;
Love that was earthly wings - its flight to holier places;
The dead are sacred things - that multiply our graces.

They, whom we loved on earth - attract us now to heaven;
Who shared our grief and mirth - back to us now are given;
They move with noiseless feet - gravely and sweetly round us;
And their soft touch hath cut - full many a chain that bound us.

Oh! dearest dead - to Heaven - with grudging sighs we gave you;
To Him, be doubts forgiven - who took you there to save you;
Now give us grace to love - your memories yet more kindly;
Pine for our homes above - and trust to God more blindly.

F.W. Faber

Chapter Eleven

SELF DEPENDENCE

Weary of myself and sick of asking
What I am, and what I ought to be:
At this vessel' s prow I stand
which bears me
Forwards, forwards, o' er the starlit sea.

By Matthew Arnold.

Yes, I would be going over the starlit sea, but it wouldn't be by ship, but by plane.

After mother's funeral Victor had invited us to visit him in Canada. It was then July. He had to return to Vancouver as he had work to do in a hospital. We agreed on September, being a lovely month. The family were enthusiastic, and I really felt I needed a holiday. As Roger couldn't get leave, that left Louise, Anthony and myself.

We would be going for one month. The next few weeks were hectic. Passports to be checked, currency, travellers cheques and a flight to be booked. I arranged for a sitting with Doris Collins at the College of Psychic Studies.

"Your husband is saying get your papers in order," she said.

"I have," I replied.

"Well check again - he is most insistant."

After a few more messages I left. On arriving home the first thing I did was to check through all my papers, and was glad I did, as it dawned on me that I had forgotten to apply for the visa from the American Embassy to enable us to pass from Canada through to the U.S.A. So Stan had known, how wonderful- but then he was always meticulous - so why should he change now? I sat down and wrote to

75

the Embassy in London immediately. I received a form a week later. Was I coloured? With whom would I be staying, and where? For how long? Who else would accompany me? etc, etc.

A few weeks later we left. It was a long flight. I had many hours to think, and spent my time just looking out of the window. I was glad to be going on holiday but wished Stan were with me - my first ever without him. Louise and Anthony were reading. The feeling of leaving the earth is always a little awesome and being entombed in a steel contraption, at the mercy of the elements, can be a sobering thought. Looking out of the window I saw miles and miles of snow. I became mesmerized. Greenland, someone said. After six hours I had the feeling I wanted to get out! We touched down at Alberta for refuelling - then on again. I looked around, and saw couples talking and knew I would never have the pleasure of having Stan sitting next to me - not on this earth anyway.

It was a good flight, but we were all glad to land. Victor was waiting for us at Vancouver. A short drive brought us to his luxury flat, lit up at night around a swimming pool, shrubs and plants. It was a welcoming sight. We all slept well that night. The following days went quickly by. Two lovely parks were visited, Queen Elizabeth and Stanley Park. We saw the majestic Lions Gate Bridge which spanned the gap between Stanley Park and the North Shore, the brilliance of the border flowers and shrubs in constant evidence along the many paths and driveways. We saw the imposing Mount Olympus after driving across the border into America - where deer came right up to us feeding from our hands. The second week we took the ferry to Vancouver Island, where we had lunch in another lovely park, and visited that endearing piece of architecture known as 'Fable Cottage' - a real fairy-tale cottage with topsy-turvy furniture, a child's dream. The man who designed it was supposed to be an eccentric, be this as it may, it drew tourists by the hundreds.

One evening Victor invited some friends in for supper. They were a Polish doctor, his wife and two sons. I cooked the meal. We were invited back to their house in Vancouver where his wife cooked a part of a large moose which the doctor had shot whilst in the north of Canada. It tasted like roast beef only much sweeter. Beautifully cooked, but not entirely to my taste. She later invited us to her Palm

Springs home which we later visited. It reminded me of a doll's house town. What struck me was the absence of neighbours talking to each other over gardens. It seemed deserted. Huge air-conditioned limousines drew up outside fabulous super-markets, smart women entered shops, reappeared with the most expensive fruits and foods and drove quietly away. I saw no groups idly talking as one does in British towns, or in Europe where old people sit on benches watching the rest of the world go by. Although the weather was exceptionally hot (120 degrees F) I found shop assistants a trifle cool - it didn't seem a friendly place to me. We were very glad though to swim in the pool behind her house, although the water was very warm and one did not feel at all refreshed after a swim. We must have jumped into the pool half a dozen times in an hour, but felt just as lethargic. The weather was just too hot to do anything. Even eating was no enjoyment as no one felt hungry. One evening we all went out for a meal at a new restaurant. Here again we did not enjoy it. The meal was awful, the meat hardly cooked. I left mine.

The following morning I decided I had had enough, and mentioned that I would love to visit the Grand Canyon before returning home. The doctor's wife said it was a five hour journey by Greyhound Bus. After having lived in South Africa for six years and seen so many wonderful places, I was totally unprepared for my first glimpse of the Canyon. It is unforgettable. I would say that the Grand Canyon in Arizona is the first natural wonder of the world. It has been put as the eighth. The chasm is 217 miles in length and a mile deep, formed by the Colorado River and it's tributaries, forced to cut deeper and deeper into a slowly rising plateau. Scientists have said it has taken millions of years to make the Canyon, where rains, winds and frost have sculpted huge bluffs and towering rocks. It is still going on.

The Colorado River being the second largest in the United States is about 2,000 miles. Measured at the gauging station at Grand Canyon, nearly half a million tons of sand and silt are carried away every twenty-four hours, by the power of its swift currents.

The Greyhound Bus dropped us and the rest of the passengers outside one of the lodges, the Blue Angel Lodge, where we were very lucky to find that there were a few vacancies. We should have booked, as many tourists visit this most spectacular place, only we hadn't decided to come until the last day at Palm Springs. The Blue Angel Lodge was only about 50 feet away from one of the trails descending to the Canyon, the Blue Angel trail. Visitors can walk or hire a donkey - it is quite steep and tourists are warned to take plenty of water. It can be extremely hot in summer. Major John Powell made the first exploration of the Canyon in 1869, by navigating the Colorado River in small boats. It wasn't until 1908 that the Canyon was made a National Monument.

During the day a guide would take tourists along the trails examining local flowers and answering questions. At night there was a film show on the Canyon and the many animals living there. A booklet which I read whilst at the Canyon stated there are 60 species of mammals, 180 species of birds, 25 reptiles and 5 amphibians living there, and what is extremely interesting is that there are some evolutionary differences for the South and North Rim, due to their separation by the great chasm for such a long time period.

It was populated long before the arrival of the white man. Hundreds of prehistoric Indian ruins are scattered around the area. It is said there are five Indian tribes who live in the Canyon region. These are the Havasupai, Hopi, Hualpai, Navajo, and Paiute.

In the year 1540 the Canyon was discovered by the first white man, a Lopez de Cardenas. Half a million tourists visit the Canyon yearly. I was happy just to sit and watch the changing colours of the rocks from rose coloured at sunrise to gold at midday and to see the setting sun at night from Mohave Point. We did not have enough time to see everything we wished to see, but I would dearly love to go again. Next time to see the Petrified Forest and the Painted Desert, which is quite near to U.S. Highway 66. Here can be seen a giant logo of brilliantly coloured agate which cover the ground in confusion. I bought some small stones for myself in the Lodge's curio shop. Agate (Silicon Dioxide) Petrified Wood from Arizona, Snowflake Obsidian from Utah and Howlite, also a small piece of Jade from Wyoming.

The last day at the Canyon we treated ourselves and hired a small six-seater plane which flew over the Canyon. Louise madly taking photos as we turned and dived. We later heard that a man and his two sons were killed in their small plane flying over the Canyon. Some fly so low it is a wonder more aren't killed. A tourist took a snap of Louise and I with the pilot of the plane. He looked tired as he had been flying non-stop all that morning. It had been a marvellous week.

We had arranged to go back by Greyhound Bus, passing the magnificent Hoover Dam and Las Vegas, the lights of which we could see over twenty miles away. We arrived at 4 o'clock in the morning where flashing neon signs bewildered us with their colours and shapes. People were still playing at the casinoes. This was a sham world after the one we had seen. Over fed, over indulgent man, where money by whatever means was the important factor.

Our holiday was over and we were back on the aircraft. Victor drove us to the airport. After a few months he left Canada for good and settled in England.

We beheld a beautiful sunset on our arrival at Heathrow, which was more spectacular than those seen at the Canyon. Arriving home I found a letter on the mat from Joan, whom I had known since the age of fourteen. She had joined the W.A.A.F.'s during the war and had married the Squadron Leader of Manston Airfield. As he was a Canadian he naturally wanted to go back to his own country and family. We had not met for years. The letter said they had lived in Toronto, but had now decided to move and had bought a lovely house on Vancouver Island, and if ever I wanted to go for a holiday I could. If only she had written that letter a few weeks before, I would have loved to have seen her, as the quaint little 'Fable Cottage' was only a stone's throw away from her new home.

I did not know when I would be visiting Canada again. The fare being the only obstacle. If I started saving now, I could be back in five years!!

Her next letter was at Christmas. They hoped to be in England the following August, as her husband would be attending a conference in London. Joan and I could meet then. I hadn't seen her husband since their wedding. I do like to keep up with old friends.

Chapter Twelve

REACHING INTO THE UNKNOWN

I lie in a heavy trance
with a world of dream without me;
Shapes of shadow dance
in wavering band about me;
but at times, some mystic things
appear - in this phantom lair;
That almost seems to me visitings
of truth known elsewhere.
The world is wide, these things are small;
they may be nothing, but they are all.

By Lord Loughton.

Many times during our holiday I had 'sensed' Stan was with me, even imagining I saw mystic things and shadows dancing. This was quite easy to imagine sitting in the moonlight overlooking the Canyon. As old as time itself. Weird and wonderful. Louise and I were up at sunrise where we hoped to see the sun rise over the rim of the crater, and again at sunset - where other tourists also gathered. The stars rocks and gorges were indescribable. Once I had settled down after our holiday I again visited Dorothy's home circle. Here Florrie read a short extract from Waldo Trine's 'In Tune With the Infinite' - a wonderful book. I wished I had taken it on holiday.

We are told that by seeking with wisdom we are reaching out of the spirit into the Great Unknown - which can be a wonderful adventure. No person is too old to learn. We can strengthen the vibrations between earth and spirit - in other words to form a bond between the two worlds. The desire to help others by bringing to them this knowledge is a gift of the spirit! It is a sad state of affairs when many refuse to believe in God or people's idea of God, simply because sorrow has overtaken them. The spirit world have told us that they cannot shut out our troubles which come our way, but they can and will strengthen us and will help us to solve our difficulties. They tell us Earth is a great training ground, and one's journey through it should be used for the purpose of dividing the earth and spirit. One, to keep the earth in it's proper place, and two, to train spirit for the great work ahead. To be able to live on earth yet be one with spirit. We have all been gifted in one way. Not one person has been left out. For one to have brains and not use them is a crime, to use those brains to commit a crime is also a crime. They should be used for the betterment of the person or mankind. Every action will have to be answered for one day.

It was time for clairvoyance which was always held in a small room. Individuals went in separately. The message I had that afternoon from Stan was, "To Thine Oneself Be True" and "it must follow as night follows day that thou cans't be false to any man." He was quoting from Shakespeare. I never cared for Shakespeare. But this made sense. We never had any of Shakeapeare's plays in our home, but all the works of Dicken's, George Elliott and Jane Austin.

Florrie asked if there were any questions I wished to ask Stan. There were so many I didn't know where to begin. I asked if it were possible for him to 'appear to me.' She said he would appear when the time was right, if I sat and meditated each afternoon at a certain time. There had to be enough power in a room for this to take place. Apparently something which the sitter gives off. I took this to be electrical energy. It was necessary for me to be calm, hence meditation, which calms the mind, and should shut off the outside world.

"Keep on with the search," he told Florrie, and "I am with her all the way."

Stan said, "The children have more common sense. It doesn't matter what the Church thinks. We have this love between us. My case will come up in April." (The inquest on Stan's accident).

Florrie then said that there was an uncle John who wished to communicate. This was my favourite uncle. He said, "If only Lily knew how close I am to her." His wife Lily was my aunt who was quite inconsolable after his death. I wrote and told her, also the hymn played at his funeral, which he stressed he would like me to tell her. This I did in a letter, saying I would come and visit her, even though it was a three hour journey. She lived next door to where my mother had lived. All our relations lived near to each other. Her answer to my letter made me gasp when I had read it. I was told if I should go and see her, the door would be slammed in my face. Someone must have spoken to her as I had always liked my aunt, and we got on so well. This must have been a person in the Anglican Church, not that she went for a long time. Why do people think other people are always right, hadn't she a mind of her own? She, like me had had a wonderful marriage. Uncle John was like Stan, dependable, kind, and liked by all. I had shared my experiences with her, but she preferred to listen to an outsider. She never wrote or spoke to me again after this. Not only was I sad at this, but uncle John was upset too, as he knew he would never be able to get through now. This had been a golden opportunity for her, and I can only blame Church people for this with their bigoted ideas and narrow mindedness. Far better if they had only been quiet. If aunt Lily could be helped then she could pass on the good news. It makes more impact if each person can relay their own experiences.

I also had a message for my vicar from a relation of his wife's. Naturally he did not believe it, but I was asked to please tell him. I had been reading the Arthur Findlay books, which I lent him. It wasn't until a few months later that what Florrie said came true. I was sitting quietly in my lounge at three o'clock when it seemed as if a mist had built up. Outside it was cold and windy. An outline seemed to be building up in the mist, at first a faint figure appeared, then more clearly. It could only be Stan. I recognised the shape of his head, his face, but what was more startling was that he was wearing his cardigan which I had bought him one birthday. When I mentioned the fact to friends later - (the few I had left in the Anglican Church) they asked if I saw the cardigan in colour. I said I had not. They then asked me how I recognised it. I replied I had recognised it by the pattern of the stitch which was a cable pattern. It was unbelieveable but nevertheless true. I had bought it so I should know it. I know they didn't believe, but my friends in the Spiritualist church believed.

83

I mentioned this to Florrie at our next meeting, and said I tried to speak but was so surprised that I could not. She said that Stan was trying so hard to concentrate but would do better next time. She said that spirit was drawing us closer to each other. He was handing me a diamond ring for purity (diamond was my birth stone) to prove to me. The reason Stan was wearing the cardigan I bought him was that it was actually him, and this was proof. Secondly, thoughts are 'things' in the world of spirit, and they can clothe themselves in the garments of their choice. (The very thing my friend told me at our first meeting, when she encountered her father). Many books have been written on this subject. Electromagnetism is involved in all types of psychic phenomena, associated with the spirit body, whether co-existent with the physical body or after. Both the spirit world and our world are wrapped up together - interpenetrate and penetrate.

Florrie said Stan wasn't in the lower planes, and where he is there is a pretty garden with a small bridge and clear river, no mud, no dirt, and he can see my reflection in the water.

To those who have no idea what the lower planes are, I have copied a few paragraphs from Chapter Nine of 'The Return of Arthur Conan Doyle,' edited by Ivan Cooke. I was so impressed by this book I bought it for my vicar. He seemed interested, and I hoped he would eventually believe. He did believe but not until a long time later!!

'THE ASTRAL WORLDS'
as relayed by spirit, from chapter nine
as mentioned above:-

"There are indeed astral worlds encompassing this, each in a differing state of vibration from coarser to finer. 'Encompassing' is the word, for they are not distant planets like Mars or Venus, but are additional departments or colonies of this world, which they encase - much as an onion is encased by its various skins, and yet also interpenetrate our world with themselves, much as water soaks through a sponge.

These astral worlds are mostly of a higher vibration than the physical, and therefore consist of a finer matter. Human life is less burdened since the astral body worn over there by man does not

84

weigh down its wearer, but is a thing of beauty, health and joy. This is the Summerland beloved by Spiritualists. Souls go there (souls being humans freed from the flesh but otherwise unchanged) and inhabit an astral body. They do not at once become greatly wise or spiritual. Rest and refreshment after the toils of their earth life is the first necessity. This they obtain, and they remain in the astral world while time slips past.

Some will say this is too good to be true. Nothing is too good to be true. Therefore it is perhaps a pity wilfully to believe, habitually to believe, in things too bad to be true, of which there are many varieties, most of which are only bogies. But if people find this makes them happy, well why not? What matters to us is that the astral worlds are very close to us always; becauae they interpenetrate our world and even influence our daily life, whether we are conscious or unconscious of the fact.

Because these worlds are so close, the majority of spiritualistic contacts are with people of the astral, who are little changed from their former selves, except that their life is more serene than ours, less limited, less burdened, and their world more beautiful. They are not greatly wise, and their message lacks power. Great things are not demanded of those living in the restful Summerland.

There is, unfortunately, another side to the picture. We have considered the higher astral wee worlds (or planes, to be more accurate). But what of those of a slower, of a lower vibration; perhaps even lower than this earth? These are not pleasant places for they are peopled by humans whose lives have attuned them to such places. They are grey, misty, dark November-fog places, good to get out of. That is why they exist; to spur their folk to get away, by their own spiritual efforts. Some are worse even than the November-fog plane, but it does no good to try to frighten people into goodness. The Church tried out this method for centuries without success. Hence the decline in the popularity of hell-fire preaching.

Whither is all this leading us? To a better understanding of the (birthday) message of Arthur Conan Doyle, when he said that 'to be cleared from astral ties wasn't altogether an easy matter.' This was surely an understatement when it meant so great an act, so great a surrender, on his part. For at that moment he must have relinquished

*his promised Summerland of rest, refreshment and recreation which
was due after his strenuous years. Yet, in the Summerland life there
is an element of forgetfulness, even of heedlessness of the cry of pain
rising from men - that 'cry which hath no language but a cry!' For
Arthur Conan Doyle there could be no forgetfulness, no laying down
of his burden, no sealing of the heart. A new dedication, a new
crusade was waiting to establish a new truth, since the earlier truth
for which he had formerly labourerd proved insufficient.*

*Therefore he said, 'In a broad sense the seeds of thought that he
(man) sows are interpreted as actions; but now I find that thought is
more powerful than action, since one of the first things a man is faced
with on his escape from earth life is a world of his own thoughts."*

'The Return of Arthur Conan Doyle' by Ivan Cooke was given to me
by my friend Vivienne after Stan's accident, and every page is worth
reading, with much information on spirit life.

Chapter Thirteen

PSYCHIC PHENOMENA

After reading books on psychic phenomena I was extremely pleased to be told that a seven day course was being held at Stansted Hall, Essex. One had to book immediately as the courses were popular. This I did.

Stansted Hall is an imposing building set in large grounds, once owned by Arthur Findlay who was a devout Spiritulalist, and on his death he left it for the advancement and study of psychic studies. Beautifully cared for and elegant with portraits of the Findlay family, with polished floors and large windows overlooking grounds of trees, shrubs, and whilst I was there masses of daffodils.

A small museum in the grounds contained many unusual exhibits. One being a photo of a young girl holding a fairy in her hand. (This was one of the Cottingley fairies investigated by Sir Arthur Conan Doyle over sixty-five years ago). Two young girls had actually seen and photographed the fairies. The parents sent it to Kodak where it was developed, to everyone's surprise it was apparent that here was no ordinary photograph. The girls said it was genuine. This made headlines. Many however said they were frauds, and Sir Arthur was asked for his opinion. Kodak said the negatives were genuine. So did Conan Doyle. I wondered if Sir James Barrie's book 'Peter Pan' was based on his sightings of these tiny creatures. He was educated at Edinburgh University, later to be Rector. Scots are very psychic, and he must have had much time in which to meditate on the huge grassy hill overlooking the town - before the coming of television and the jet age. If he did see them he didn't let on, as anything psychic was against the Church's beliefs.

The course, 'Physical Phenomena in Theory and Practice,' was given by the Principal, Mr Gordon Higginson, M.S.N.U. A charming man, well educated and intellectual, also well liked. The first three days we had talks and lectures and demonstrations of clairvoyance. I had taken my tape-recorder in the hope of receiving a message. Seated in the front row I was the first to receive one.

Gordon came straight to me saying, "Your husband is here and says you have four children - is that correct?"

"Yes," I said delightedly, as this was further proof from another stranger who didn't know my affairs. Proof for friends and family. (I did not now need proof myself of course).

Gordon went on.

"You have a daughter in France?"

"Yes that is correct," I said.

He was an extremely good medium as Louise had left for France a few months previous, working as an au pair.

"I see her working in a shop putting tins on a shelf," he said.

I hesitated as she was not working in a shop. I didn't contradict him as something told me not to. Gordon then told me that my husband was telling him the names of my children. He then said that Stan was so glad to be able to come back and speak to me. I had everything on tape and was overwhelmed by the message. Others also received good messages, and he received a great ovation at the end of the afternoon.

Before the evening meal I walked in the grounds and thought about the messages. He only got one part wrong, about Louise working in a shop, but that wasn't important.

Mornings started with meditation, and healing for those who needed it in the Sanctuary, followed by breakfast in the large dining-room. Then lectures until lunch. A huge library for those wishing to learn about the mechanics of mediumship and philosophy prevented anyone becoming bored in the evenings.

Two days before the course ended Gordon held a seance in a special room he only kept for psychic phenomena. People were asked to remove all jewellery, watches, lighters etc., before entering the room. About sixty people entered the room and the door was locked. It is extremely unnerving for a medium to be interrupted during a seance. After about ten minutes quiet meditation with only a dim red light in the room Gordon went into trance. He was sitting in a circle surrounded by other experienced mediums, all of whom were giving power to the seance. Then a spirit voice was heard asking that the red light be turned down a little, as the spirit-people could not operate in a bright light if they want to get down to earth's vibrations. First Gordon's control came through. It was a child's voice and the child was called 'Cuckoo' - it sounded like a Yorkshire accent. Then another voice with a strong Scots brogue. This was a man's voice. He was known as Paddy. Paddy took charge completely. It was he who announced that the spirit people coming through would be to those in the room and would the people please acknowledge them. It was a big effort for some of them to come.

First to materialise was Gordon's old Chinese guide, he walked slowly around the room. Spirits cannot come through without the aid of a human body, it is the etheric body which is 'taken over.' A white mist suddenly emerged, called ectoplasm, this slowly built up into a human form. The guide took about five minutes to slowly walk around the circle, then gradually dematerialised.

Then Paddy announced in his strong voice that a man was trying to 'get through' to a lady. He in fact had only passed on that week, and was annoyed that he hadn't been buried! There was much laughter at that. Paddy then announced the name of the man who had died. I heard a gasp at my side and it came from the lady sitting on my left. Before the seance had begun she had confided in me that she had received a telegram from Scotland saying her brother-in-law had died and she would be going to his funeral. I said that it would be a pity to miss the course especially as she had paid so much to come, with fares from Scotland etc., in any case her brother-in-law knew she would be here on this course and he might contact her, (although I thought it too soon for any deceased person to get through).

The lady sitting on my left was infact the person who had received the telegram. Once again we saw the white ectoplasm slowly build up into a human form, and to my amazement and that of everyone in the room, the figure slowly walked towards the lady and I, and spoke to her. I know I was shaken and I know she must have been for she clutched my arm. He said hello and called her name. I think she was too shocked to answer, but Paddy told her to speak, to keep up the flow of conversation to encourage him, otherwise the ectoplasm fades away. This really was the most wonderful thing I had ever seen (apart from Stan's manifestation in my lounge). Eventually, once again the white ectoplasm faded away, leaving us all in silence.

Perhaps her brother-in-law was psychic, had known about Spiritualism and all it entailed, also he knew she would be coming to Stansted Hall, and with a lot of help from the spirit world was able to come through, but even so, it was the first time I had ever heard of a deceased person walking and talking so quickly after 'passing on.' The lady was so impressed that after the seance was over, she went around to every person in the room with a pen and paper and asked if they would write their names and addresses down as proof, as she knew no one would ever believe her.

Afterwards I spoke to her, saying I was thinking of writing a book later and would she mind if I included this. She agreed. The name of the lady was Mrs E. Dow of Edinburgh. How can the public know such things unless they read it for themselves - and witnessed by so many people. A sceptic could say of course that anyone could drape a white sheet around them. This is true, but she actually saw him, same size, height and voice. Gordon was still sitting in his chair. Mediums are the first to be suspected of fraud, and Gordon has had his share like other famous mediums of the day. The door had been locked. Also, as Gordon was in a deep trance, he had no idea who was 'coming through' - it is the control who does the speaking - the words do not come from Gordon's mind. He is only there to be 'used' by the spirit world.

I hoped her relations believed her, but some are so bogged down with their own prejudices that they cannot think with a clear mind. I have noticed those who are most against spirit messages are the church people, of various denominations, Anglicans, Catholics, Baptists, Evangelists, and Jehovah's Witnesses, and they take it out on us by coming in to our churches, destroying hymn books, and smashing windows, this terrible behaviour was apparent in the north of England some time ago. People holding banners trying to prevent Spiritualists from attending services, or Psychic Fairs, amongst them vicars who are hypocrites, as they preach always about the 'Brotherhood of Man' but never practice it! This was very apparent one Sunday morning. I was listening to the Radio, a service was being broadcast from an Anglican church. The first words I heard were, "Let us pray for all Christians everywhere." A silence - then the prayers commenced. At no time were Muslims, Buddhists, or any other religions mentioned. Are they going to be denied entry to heaven just because they weren't baptised into the Christian religion? I have thought for a long time that it is a pity Christianity was ever brought to Britian. The Crusades were the most horrific example of Christianity at work. Fine men were sent thousands of miles away to kill others in their own land because they had another religion. Fine women were killed, brutally in England and throughout Europe because they were used by the spirit world to do healing and to give clairvoyant messages. Joan of Arc being one of them, or the many thousands. I always thought Christianity was a religion of peace, if it is not, then I want nothing to do with it.

We had one more day before the course ended, a medium would be giving messages to those interested in the morning. In the evening a telephone call came saying the medium was ill but she had contacted another medium who would stand in for her. This medium was a Doris Stokes. I had heard of her, a very likeable person from the north of England. She sat at our table at breakfast that morning, but as she was at the end of the table I couldn't speak to her. As usual I took my tape-recorder along, and sat in the front. She gave a short address. People had clapped as she entered the room, knowing she had only been told barely twenty four hours previously and she had come a long way. She gave several messages, then came to me.

"I have a young looking man here who was in a bad accident. He says the lorry hit him side-on. The lorry driver who caused the accident tried to pull him out. The lorry driver was much younger. He tried to put the fire out."

I felt very upset at this, she noticed, and said, "It's alright love, he's alright now and sends his love."

She also gave me a message for my vicar. I said he wouldn't believe it.

"Perhaps he won't, but you are asked by spirit to give it to him."

She then looked around asking if there was anyone by the name of Cooper. Nobody answered. I wasn't taking much notice as I had had my message and was trying to picture it in my mind. She repeated the

name Cooper, my brain suddenly came alive, and I remembered it
was Vivienne's married name.

I replied that I had a friend named Cooper, and she wanted to come,
but couldn't.

"A man is here who died quickly from a heart condition."

I said that was true, as Donald had died in the street. A few more
messages came.

"Will you please give her this message as she is still upset?"

I promised to do so. Luckily I had it all on tape.

The course ended in the afternoon. What a wonderful place, and to
witness things I never thought possible. I arrived home later that day
to find a letter on the mat from Louise in France. She was well, still
liked her job but was now doing one day part-time in a local shop, she
wanted to leave in the summer, but we were invited by her employer
to visit them before she left.

After breakfast the following day the first thing I did was to write to
Vivienne and tell her I would be coming to Birmingham to see her,
then she could hear the message for herself. I also contacted my vicar
about the message given to him - about one of his family. He didn't
believe it - as I knew he wouldn't.

The coming week I sat down and wrote in a book I kept especially
for messages, all that had happened. So Gordon Higginson was
correct when he said Louise was working in a shop. How humiliated
he would have felt if I had disagreed. We are told always to be honest
with a medium and agree only if we know the message to be true, and
yet something told me it was true. My intuition was therefore correct.
It was amazing that Gordon knew before I did!

I had also given the vicar the message, perhaps he would believe it
one day. I had kept my side of the bargain with spirit.

Roger and I had decided to go to France later in the year, and pick up
Louise who was working in Lyon. She wanted to practice her French,
and had worked in a cafe as well as being an au pair. She had missed
home and now wanted to return. I was glad, as I did not like the idea
of her being alone.

Stan's inquest came later in the month, and what Doris Stokes said
was true. For the first time I felt sorry for the young lorry driver. It
would be on his conscience for the rest of his life, and he did try to

help Stan. It was his firm's fault after all for allowing him to drive such a dangerous vehicle.

At our next circle, at Dorothy's home, I repeated everything I had seen and heard. Florrie told me to start writing. I did so, then tore up the sheets of paper, I couldn't see anyone becoming even faintly interested in my story. Then I remembered how Bishop Pike's experiences had helped me, not forgetting the wonderful messages I had from mediums. Perhaps it may bring a glimmer of hope to someone to realise there is always someone on the 'other side' wishing to help us.

People will say I have been unjust to the clergy. Well I have had good cause. What I condemn is their ignorance and utter refusal to give their time to try and learn about the 'other world' which they speak of continually, until the moment of death when they want to forget. To me they are like a lot of frightened sheep who lack the courage to enquire - so naturally their flock follow. They talk always of miracles, so they should be interested in 'The Return of Arthur Conan Doyle' Chapter III (as told by the spirit world) on the feeding of the five thousand, and *how* it was done.

Chapter Fourteen

TO LET GO

One by one bright gifts from heaven
Joys are sent thee here below;
Take them readily when given
Ready too to let them go

By Adelaide Anne Proctor.

It was now 1978 and the family were all finding their feet, and I had to be prepared to let them go.

Angela continued with nursing at her local hospital. Roger was now engaged as a courier by a firm in France who rented out mobile homes. Louise was allowed to accompany him on her holiday as a helper. She was keen to learn photography and was studying for her degree in technical photography. Shortly before she left for France, we were walking in my garden when I spotted an orange-red flower in the middle of my lawn. Louise asked me why I had planted a flower right in the middle of the lawn. I said I hadn't planted any flower, and had never had any geums, and it certainly wasn't there yesterday. Then I remembered it was the 1st July - the anniversary of my mother's death - and she had loved geums, especially the orange-red ones. But how it came to be there was a mystery. I went around all the gardens the following day just to see if any of the neighbours had grown any - maybe a stray seed had found it's way on to my lawn, but I did not see any geums. I dug it up and placed it by my rockery, and was delighted to see it thrive, in fact I have never seen such a tall geum.

Anthony was now a steward on British Airways and went on a six week course. His main aim was to become a pilot. In August that year

French air traffic controllers went on strike putting extra pressure on air-lines. Airports were filled to over-flowing. Airport staff were praised. Anthony made trips to New York, Dubai, Singapore and Australia and always looked tired when he returned.

I joined Louise and Roger in France later as I had the opportunity of purchasing a mobile home in that area. I spent two weeks holiday in the mobile home on Roger's site and made friends with an English lady who occupied the mobile home next to me. One day we were sitting outside talking when a telegram arrived for her. I could tell it was bad news as she gave a startled cry. Her husband had just died. I made her a cup of tea and I asked her if she would like me to help her tidy up her mobile home as she would have to catch a plane back to England. She was in such a state of shock that I helped her to pack and found someone to take her to the airport. Strangely enough we had been talking about Spiritualism and all it entailed that day. I gave her a book which I thought might help her. We said good-bye and she promised to write.

When I arrived home from France I found a letter on the mat thanking me for the book which had helped her. Perhaps I was meant to go on holiday at that time and at that particular place.

I decided also to let go of old church acquaintances as I now realised we had nothing whatsoever in common. People who I had once thought of as friends now crossed the road when I appeared - not because of any rift between us - but simply because I had found comfort and enlightenment in another church. That this was a Spiritualist church made it all the more shocking as it went against all their teachings. I emphasise their teachings, not the Bible's teachings! Spiritualism is openly encouraged in the New Testament by St. Paul, (healing and prophesy being considered the greatest of gifts). One would expect the clergy to agree, but no, they would rather believe in the Old Testament, records of which go back hundreds of years before Christ. Spiritualists know by heart the well worn phrase that, 'thou must not suffer a witch to live,' but who is the witch? Perhaps people in high places were put in their place by the so-called witches, and gave messages which would cause shame and even embarrassment. These witches being mediums, who only gave messages as they received them, had to be got rid of and quick. It was probably the high priests who made the rules to save their positions in society. It certainly couldn't be God's wishes to kill these mediums as firstly, they were only using the powers given to them, and secondly, if it were true that God gave the ten commandments to Moses on tablets of stone, for all people for all time, one of the ten being 'Thou shalt not kill,' then the Priests had deliberately disobeyed an order, and had taken the law into their own hands! The clergy today still take the law into their own hands. Since women are now ordained into the Church of England many clergy cannot accept this, and rather than keep their vows are actually willing to switch to the Catholic faith. This shows a meanness of spirit. They are also letting down their own congregations by their petty behaviour. In ancient Egypt and Greece women had high positions and today in Britain there are far more women than men who are mediums. Our churches are filling whilst theirs are declining. The bereaved are the ones who are suffering the most as they are not being comforted. They are made to feel guilty if they should even think they would love to hear from a loved one who has departed this life.

This brings me to another message - quite important to my way of thinking - from Florrie at our next circle meeting. The message was simple, not full of philosophy or religious overtones which I would have expected.

"Do you know a vicar who has passed over? said Florrie.

"Yes," I replied. "A vicar in South Africa who died ten year's ago." Florrie shook her head.

"No, I am speaking of a much more recent death."

I said I didn't know of any other vicar who had died.

"Oh well, he is just saying how tall your runner beans are, and by the way he understands everything now."

In bed that evening I went over and over again the message given to me. That year I had decided to grow runner beans for the first time in my life. I took a great deal of trouble and grew them in the conservatory so that they could have a good start. I was amazed how tall they grew, much taller than any the neighbours had. It was the latter part of the message I didn't understand.

I did understand though the following morning. I had a short letter from Betty informing me that our vicar had died, the vicar from whose church I had left in desperation. I was genuinely sorry as I had liked him and his whole family. There again, we had crossed words because I couldn't agree with the teachings of his Church and went my own way. Now it seems he had come back to my way - and he understands everything now. Of course, it could only mean one thing. He now realised what I had been telling him all along, that a person does survive death and the spirit lives on. He must have really eaten humble pie to have come back to me of all people. I couldn't help saying, "Well, I told you so." I felt sorry though for his wife who would have loved a message but wouldn't go to a medium knowing how her church viewed them. There is something sinister in this, when a person is frightened into doing something for fear of being punished, by whom? Also, one is not in control of their own feelings. What a pity though that he had to wait until he died before he knew the truth. He could have done so much for his congregation in times of death. I told no one of my message except Betty, who seemed very interested. It was pointless in my telling any one in my old Church - it would have been dismissed instantly. Remarks such as, "Why should he come back to you and not his wife?" Or "Poor Joyce - she should have never left our church, she must be in a terrible state."

Yes, I certainly would have been if I had continued attending the church. What a lot these narrow minded people were missing. Meanwhile I had my own life to lead.

It was whilst I was attending the 'Psychic Phenomena Course' at Stansted that I learnt that lectures and courses were held at the Spiritualists Association of Great Britain at Belgrave Square, London. I decided to go and travelled a week later, enlisting on a course in healing. I made two new friends the first month, Nellie, a healer in her own church and Eugenie, a Polish lady.

I took a great interest in all lectures and demonstrations. We three had a great deal in common. Life for me now took on a new meaning. For the first time I was amongst people who were willing to give up a lot of their spare time to find out about the different aspects of healing, the many methods used, from colour and sound to crystals. The courses were usually twelve weeks. Most important to me was the fact that everyone I met believed in the survival of the spirit, and all had received a message from someone who had passed over. There were some very good mediums there who gave private sittings or public demonstrations in the afternoons and evenings. Life was full of interest and I knew Stan was glad I had joined as he came through many times at private sittings, which I always tried to book on the day of our wedding anniversary and at Christmas. I felt as though the people in my old church were on another planet. When would they allow healing in their church I wondered. Nothing ever stands forever, and would it be possible that after standing still for two thousand years that they would permit healing. Time will tell.

The Greater World Association, in London, held a fete that summer, and we three decided to attend. I had been troubled by a cough for a few weeks and I didn't feel all that good. Mediums were giving private sittings, so I decided to book one with a Doreen Hunt. Straight away she advised me to take a certain medicine for my chest. Then to my surprise she said, "Your father is here and is sorry for the way he treated you."

I replied that my father was a good man, but it was probably my step father. He never spoke to me - or to my brother - even at Christmas. It was a miserable home. I was glad when Stan and I married and I left. It was an excellent sitting. A few days later I bought the medicine prescribed, and three weeks later my cough disappeared. When Doreen Hunt gave the message that it was my father, she said she could see a father figure. This was quite true as it was my step-father, although he had never been a father to me. Anyhow she ended the message by saying all is forgiven now!!'' The medium said he is handing you some Lily-of-the Valley. I have these in my garden. They are always out by Stan's birthday in May.

Chapter Fifteen

MAN'S INHUMANITY TO MAN
AND ANIMALS

*In the happy time to come, when the lessons have been learnt, it will
be the passing untrammelled into Spirit conditions where work in its
real sense represents your Spirit's desire.*

By Zodiac, A Priest at the temple at the time of Jesus.

The papers made dreary reading. Each day a disaster occurred.
Widespread floods in Upper Pradesh, India. In Rhodesia, an Air
Rhodesia Viscount was shot down, and whilst the shocked survivors
were walking aimlessly, they were cold-bloodedly shot at by guerrillas
from the organisation of Mr. Joshua Nkomo's Zimbabwe People's
Revolutionary Army.

Nkomo openly admitted he was responsible. There was revulsion
amongst the Rhodesians and the whole world. The weary Mr Smith,
Rhodesia's Prime Minister, received no support - from either the
USA or us. The USA wanted Smith to offer Rhodesia on a platter!
The whites stuck it out - they had seen this all before. Many however
left the country. I was disgusted Britain offered no help to Smith.
Many of our missionaries were killed at mission stations. How long
were the whites in Rhodesia expected to take this?

The world was in a mess. As well as the daily depressing news, the
TV film 'Holocaust' was shown. It pictured the thousands of Jews
massacred in concentration camps, even after forty years we were
still hearing this, and still more stories were coming out about how
brutal the Germans were to ethnic communities. They still havn't
changed. Graves in Jewish cemeteries have been desecrated in
Germany, and even in Britain. One must have a deep hatred to do

such a despicable thing. The Germans were not to be allowed to forget this, nor anyone else. New upstarts were always turning up bringing fear to their communities.

Much cruelty was also going on in experimental laboratories. My friend's daughter worked in such a place. She had to leave as she couldn't take it. Not one of the scientists could be an animal lover. Why can they not experiment on humans? This would be fair, as all tests are for the supposed benefit to humans, then let humans take part. I cannot understand why the Church keeps so quiet. A few clergy here and there have tried, but they need the support of their bishops. If the clergy in the land decided to strike this would indeed cause chaos. After all, everyone else has attempted to strike. There are several things they could do. Refuse marriages, baptisms and funerals. The grave digger could still carry on! Animals are surely worth more than a dead person. Before long Parliament would have to agree to the closing of experimental laboratories.

I was overjoyed when a Dr. Alice Heim a medical research psychologist aired her views, calling for new legislation governing psychological experimentation with animals. How can these help us? A lot, under natural conditions to see how animals cope under stress, and how a female takes care of it's young, going without food itself. These experiments can be carried out in the animal's natural habitat, they do not need to be chained or caged. I wrote many times to the 'Daily Telegraph' but never saw the letters printed. It should be made law throughout the world to abolish all experiments on live animals. There were many protests about seal pups being cruelly slaughtered on beaches in Canada which were shown on TV. This still continues. How can a man look into the beautiful eyes of a seal pup and then smash it's skull. Man is really the lowest of all animals. Who are we to put ourselves before any other creature just to enjoy a few more years of life and luxury. Many British women refuse to wear animal furs, the synthetic furs look just as good and are lighter to wear. The German women though and those in Northern Europe continue. There is no shortage of money here, where vanity rules. One day the world will wake up to find no animals, no birds, nothing of beauty. What animals are left are exploited and catch unidentifiable diseases. Foot and mouth returns in cycles which cannot be explained despite strict control of animal feed, injections and laboratory tests. We all know that gallons of insecticides are pumped indiscriminately everywhere in the world. Governments are concerned but nothing is seen to be done. While output is high this will continue, but at what risk to our health? Our food must be contaminated, but there is a lot we aren't told. Not only do we suffer but animals also. The scientists will have to pay dearly for what they have done to our planet. If not in this world - then in the next!!

Many healing centres have spiritual healing for animals, they do wonderful work, trying to undo what man has done. Even these good people who give up all their time have hostile letters and critical reports in newspapers. The fact that these healers don't administer drugs, manipulation, or in no way harm the animal (as it is *spiritual* healing) does not protect them from the abuse of their own councils. They would be a valuable asset to veterinary surgeons, as advice is given from spirit by the healer's guide. Two excellent healers, Irene and Gerald Sowter, from Reigate, Surrey have such a healing centre where people and animals are treated. I had healing many times and also attended their evenings of clairvoyance which were always packed. They have both given so much to their community over the years. I think they should be mentioned in the New Year's Honours Lists.

Chapter Sixteen

SPIRIT MESSAGES

Heav'n from all creatures hides the book of fate,
All but the page prescrib'd, their present state:
From brutes what men, from men what spirits know;
Or who could suffer being here below?

Essay on Man by Pope.

I once read of a spirit message received at Glastonbury, in the west of England. This article mentioned that Britain was one of the great spiritual centres of the world. Where then I wondered has our decency, honesty and fair play gone?

As I am interested in healing and learning about the chakras in the human body, I was to learn there are seven centres of power in the world. There are many chakras in the physical body, but only seven main ones. Glastonbury is one of the main centres of power, together with London, and Iona in Scotland. Another centre of power is situated in Tibet, another in the Holy Land, the message continued, pointing out that Britain contains some of the most sacred and holiest points of divine power on the surface of this planet. At the beginning of Creation, Britain was a land inhabited solely by the angels and devic forces and although we have had crisis after crisis, which seems as if Britain is set upon a path towards economic collapse, yet we have a purpose in the destiny of the earth. I copied this out of an article loaned to me by a friend, but would like to know more about the actual source of the message - from whence it came - how did it come - was it by automatic writing - who was the medium? Every church I am sure would be interested. The message goes on.

It is decreed that during a coming of the Christ in order to fulfil the divine plan for evolution, the seeds shall be sown for the next coming. As the next coming of the Christ has indeed been destined to take place in Britain, the Nazarene's visit to this land was intended to symbolise the next place of incarnation of the Christ Light.

By a very unusual coincidence, whilst attending a lecture, I sat next to a lady, and mentioned this article I had been reading. She then astounded me by saying that she had just been reading a book which mentioned this particular subject, the book being 'The Revelation of Ramala' by the Ramala Centre, Glastonbury. I intend to buy a copy as soon as possible.

I was feeling irritable these days. A throbbing pain in my leg made life miserable. I had heard of a Mr. John Leslie, who did psychic surgery. He lived in Brighton. On an impulse I phoned him and made an appointment. I could easily have gone to my doctor five-hundred yards away, but wanted to see psychic surgery for myself. It was October 23rd. It took me two and a half hours to reach Brighton Railway Station, then a slow taxi drive to his house. I was an hour late, and felt awful as I like to be punctual. He was very understanding, and realised I had come a long way. Mr. Leslie is a charming man and explained psychic surgery, and how his spirit doctor took over. I think it would be difficult for anyone not a Spiritualist to comprehend what was going on! Another lady was resting in an adjoining room, she had been there many times, and it gave her relief. Mr. Leslie first went into a trance, after about five minutes, he slowly stood up. His spirit doctor took over, and spoke. I was lying on a table prepared for patients, and felt my head massaged, then I was asked where the pain was. I told the doctor where the throbbing was. After a brief examination and talking (between the doctor and other unseen helpers) I felt the skin of my right leg as if it were being cut quite a long way, no pain, but a definite sensation. I was told some fatty tissue had caused this throbbing. This was removed. It was really amazing. I felt pin pricks when the skin was sewn together again. No blood, no pain whatsoever, but I definitely felt something. I was told my feet would not become so numb in cold weather. Whilst the operation was in progress - about five minutes in all I suppose - the spirit doctor was talking all the time - sometimes to me, but mostly to his spirit helpers.

A most remarkable experience. The psychic surgery was performed on my astral body, but even so I still had to take care of my leg. No heavy shopping, and rest for a week or so. The awful throbbing ceased. I have no doubt I would have had to go into hospital for a week or two if I had not decided to go to Mr. Leslie, as well as the ordeal which accompanies any operation. Would I have gone I wonder, if I had known nothing about Spiritualism and spirit healing? After a rest in Mr. Leslie's house, he made me tea and then kindly drove me back to the station. He asked nothing for his services, but it would be churlish to take up his time - which he gave daily to help people - and give nothing in return. I would have paid for a private doctor so why not a spirit healer who had performed the same operation in a fraction of the time - without any pain, nor fuss but with the same care and attention. Not to mention the mistakes one sometimes reads on patients in hospitals. The following day I wrote and thanked him, saying my leg felt much better and enclosed ten pounds.

Upon arriving home, I could not wait to tell friends. I needn't have bothered. My Spiritualist friends quite naturally accepted what I told them, but it was the others who infuriated me. Two of my neighbours were ever complaining. One really did need help. She already looked like a corpse. The other had a bad eye condition. Yet when I mentioned that I would accompany them to Brighton, once they had arranged their appointments, they said that nothing would make them go. To the neighbour with the eye condition who was nearly blind, I said she had nothing to lose anyway, as the hospital could do no more for her. This was another reason for writing this book. How can the average person know until they read it for themselves? The books that could help them, such as 'The Spiritual Healer' have to be ordered. I have never seen one on a bookstall in a railway station.

My aunt also needed healing, suffering with cataracts. She had to wait months before being admitted to hospital. When I again mentioned spiritual healing she also refused. I remember going with her to her church one Sunday when the vicar said, "A Christian is one who is never afraid, never superstitious, trusting always in God." Would he have trusted in God, I thought, if he also suffered with cataracts and had decided to visit a spiritual healer. The healer also trusts in God, and knows he cannot do any healing without that power and energy flowing through him. The main trouble with most clergy is that they don't think a mere man is entitled to have healing power. The fact that many healings are done throughout Britain, and in the world daily, by ordinary men and women without knowledge of medicine leaves them unimpressed. They believe that Jesus and he alone can perform miracles. Sour grapes could enter into this. A doctor who has spent a hard five year study in medical school will naturally resent anyone who claims to heal without ever opening a medical book. Healers understand, but they are quite willing to work with them, and the guide of the healer, who in many cases were doctors before they passed to spirit, can give valuable information to the doctor, referring to treatment of the patient without the use of drugs which dull the brain and poison the system.

Many GP's were glad to visit Harry Edwards, who ran his own healing Sanctuary in Shere, Surrey many years ago. It is still a healing Sanctuary where thousands have been helped. As this knowledge grows, more and more doctors will seek the help of our healers, who can not only help them, but also our overworked National Health Service. The result could be a Britain disease free. It is not impossible if more healing centres were opened, and paid for by the Government, and the healers paid also.

The Church tells us that man cannot live by bread alone, he cannot live without bread either, so the healers must be paid, with lists kept of all successful healings. The National Federation of Spiritual Healers are very strict about this and give courses on healing on how to treat patients and what is expected of them. I have attended their courses, and one is expected to know about the healing centres in the body. Healing with colour is also bound up with this. It would be an added asset if a nurse, or a person with a good knowledge of first aid, were to attend these lectures. With their knowledge of anatomy they should be good healers. They will also find that their modern way of healing is not always thought to be the best by the workers in spirit. At the circle I attend a person is advised to take some medicant - usually herbs - and one was even told that what she was using was no good! We are advised to take a certain thing, but one always has free will and can still decide for himself. Many healers believe that one has to change one's thinking to be healthy. Evil comes not of God, neither disease nor any of the ills of Man. All that is of darkness is of Man, because he fosters the seeds of darkness in his nature. This is done in ignorance, stupidity, indolence but especially selfishness. Once rid of these a man must feel a better person and is half way to self-healing (which can be accomplished by those determined enough). Plato once said, "The greatest mistake physicians make is that they attempt to cure the body without attempting to cure the mind."

This Greek philosopher born 428 BC must have been a spiritual healer or a person very highly evolved spiritually.

The seven deadly sins - envy, lust, pride, covetousness, gluttony, sloth and anger can and do upset every cell in the body. It is like taking a deadly dose. Continual negative and bad thoughts are also poison to the system and we will suffer. People are their worst enemies. Some dwell on trifling worries distracted by their emotions, not trying to rise above them. They will not and can not relax.

Chapter Seventeen

DARKNESS

A day of clouds and darkness,
A day of wrath and woe!
The war of elements above - the strife of men below!
Thro' the air rings shout and outcry,
Thro' the streets a red tide pours,
To the booming of the cannon the ancient city roars;
For wilder than the tempest is human passion's strife,
And deadlier than the elements - the waste of human life.

By J.M. Neale.

It was a day of cloud and darkness indeed for the beginning of the year 1980. The world was in despair. Eight thousand feet up in the blizzard-whipped mountains of the Hindu Kush, eighty miles from Kabul, capital of Afghanistan, Soviet tanks, and armour were everywhere. Some Russian soldiers were in white snow suits. They were however not getting it their own way. They were getting opposition from the guerillas in the rugged terrain. A strategic highway to the north-west was being contested by Moslem rebels much opposed to Russia's intervention. Bamian, although occupied by the Russians, was encircled by rebels who had cut off supply routes. Reports had come in of tribesmen setting themselves alight with petrol and throwing themselves on the advancing Russian tanks.

This was indeed a grim start to the New Year. With rising costs in gas, electricity, petrol, bread, eggs, milk and television licences, there was little enough to celebrate as people drank their New Year toasts. The teenager paid little heed to the news, and went to parties, but the

111

older folk were worried that was this going to lead to a third world war? President Carter of America was very quick to cut all grain supplies to Russia, this was followed by Australia, who rejected the request by Russia not to cut its wheat sales. Canada had already undertaken not to increase grain shipments to the Soviet Union. How long could Russia hold out? Russia was not likely to let go quickly of something once obtained. The whole world was against her. The tribesmen learnt to handle guns at the age of ten and would fight to the last man. It was a very worrying start to the year, and not many remembered St. Paul's words,"Neither death, nor life, nor angels, nor principalities, nor powers, nor things present, nor things to come, nor height, nor depth, nor any other creature, shall be able to separate us from the love of God."

It was only in the churches that these words were read. Russia had no conscience, and cared little for the feelings of the rest of the world. Referring back to the words of St. Paul, death then should not unduly worry us if we know that another more joyous life awaits us, but even some clergy doubted this as in a recent public opinion poll to test British beliefs on spiritual matters.

The magazine 'Now' published the result of this incredible survey:

100% of all Roman Catholic Priests accepted the after life.

99% of Church of England ministers accepted the after life.

80% of Catholic people believed in the after life.

50% of Church of England people believed in the after life.

One question which was asked was:

"Do you believe the soul lives on, although the body dies?"

19% of the Roman Catholic priests said "Yes."

50% of the Church of England clergy said "Yes."

Sixty-two per cent of the Roman Catholic clergy still maintained that you go to heaven - or hell, forever! Not one Roman Catholic priest believed in reincarnation. Only one percent of Church of England ministers believed in reincarnation. When asked about the existence of God, surprisingly, of the clerics interviewed, eleven percent did NOT BELIEVE!

A further sixteen percent did not KNOW! So, given these figures were correct, is it any wonder that there is so much confusion, and people are hazy and mixed up. If the clergy cannot agree, then the people will lose faith. To me it is a wonder people still attend church, if the priests are so divided. A good experienced medium would be able to banish their doubts once and for all, but of course, a medium is the last person a priest will contact. Is it because they know deep down we are right, and they don't want to lose their congregations. After all, I left my church because of this, and there must be many like me. Is there another world or not? Will we meet our loved ones again or not? Two questions any priest should be able to answer. It is a well known fact that people who have had convincing proof do not mind dying. They know they will be reunited with their families. This is all the average person wants to know. There was not only darkness in the world, but even the Church is filled with black holes.

Chapter Eighteen

USE OF COLOUR AND SOUND IN HEALING

Music is one of God's gifts,
The sensitive soul is uplifted,
Never cease your efforts until you bring it to
respond also to purity of sound and colour.

By Mendelssohn.

Nellie and I continued to attend lectures on healing, (she was a healer in her church) but we were taught healing by the use of colour and sound.

India and China were also familiar with healing by colour, related to the laws of light connected with the seven major vibratory rays. These being red, orange, yellow, green, blue, indigo and violet. When these are used properly and understood by healers, they can cure diseases.

Many books are now being written on colour for healing, the ones which helped me were written by S.G.J. Ousely (now deceased). His book 'Colour Meditations' tells of healing as practised by the ancient Egyptians. (I thought this was a new science). He goes on to say that the mysterious people of the Nile (who worshipped the sun as a symbol of deity) also knew of the power of the solar rays to rebuild the health. The priests used bowls in which the juices of certain fruits and vegetables were first expressed, and then set them out in the sun to become charged with the 'energy of Ra' (the Sun God).

They encrusted the healing bowls with jewels of the same colour as the fruit or vegetable being used, to add a still greater potency. Nowadays, the colour healer follows the same principle by using coloured glass jars corresponding to the fruit or the rays required for the cure. In the same building where the lectures were held we sometimes saw ancient Egyptian dances being performed by a small group under the direction of a Cheryl Stoll. We always looked forward to these evenings. Haunting music would be played, with Cheryl explaining ancient Egyptian therapies, giving demonstrations to the audience. She had her own seminars, giving healing through massage, meditation and reflexology - a very gifted person. As well as the therapy acutincture, which employed powdered stones and metals, together with coloured sand to correct imbalances in the patient. All were new to me. So there is a form of healing to suit everyone these days, which is much more therapeutic than the continued use of drugs, which do not always cure and can make the patient feel worse.

We found out that Cheryl and her husband Dennis were organising a trip to Egypt later that year. Anthony's girlfriend Sally (a stewardess on British Airways) had bought me a book on Egyptian art for my birthday, with beautifully coloured illustrations. After looking at the pictures of the great tombs and temples, and the timeless art treasures, I made up my mind to join Cheryl and Dennis's tour. I was very pleased that Eugenie said she would like to go too.

It was now April, which gave me time to save up for the trip in September. The holiday would include a 600 mile cruise up the Nile, on 'The Nile Star,' arranged by Swan Hellenic.

The following months flew by until the day I dreaded arrived. I say dreaded, as I was up at the crack of dawn, went through my suitcases at least three times to make sure I had packed sun lotions, medicines etc., as we were told there would be no doctor on board, and so we should be prepared.

We all met in a London hotel where we were driven to Heathrow. I was glad to have Eugenie as a companion, as apart from Cheryl and her husband I knew no one else on the tour.

We arrived in Cairo at 2am, very humid and sticky, and were driven to a magnificent hotel. Every bedroom had a balcony overlooking the Nile - sheer luxury. Eugenie and I hoped to share a room, but in the confusion I found myself with a stranger. It was late, the staff were tired, so I put up with it. The bedrooms were huge. My companion, an elderly widow had spent most of her life in India, here again another coincidence, for she had settled in Liss, Hampshire, and was a regular visitor to the 'White Eagle' Lodge where my future son-in-law's father did healing. She knew him. So we had quite a lot in common.

There are three pyramids in Gizeh, Cheops, Chepren and Mycerinus, and this is where we were taken the following day. The Great Pyramid - or Pyramid of King Cheops is 450 ft high - truly magnificent - which commands wonder and admiration. It was while Eugenie, I, and the rest of our party were waiting to enter the Pyramid of Chephren that we saw a European emerge smoking, despite the 'No Smoking' sign in English! I was filled with shame when the old Arab squatting outside shook his head sadly. These are holy places to the Arabs. All tourists should be given lessons in etiquette before travelling to the Middle-east.

The following morning was spent visiting the Egyptian Museum, near our hotel. The ancient Egyptians were very conscious of the power of colour, and were lucky to have these precious stones at hand. There was a priceless collection here, especially Tut-ankh-Amun's Throne and his second coffin . His features were covered with a gold mask. His throne was made of carved wood covered with a sheet of gold and many colours inlaid in glass, silver, stones and majolica (enamelled pottery). I thought the back of the throne was more beautiful than the front. For here was depicted two exquisite dainty figures of the young Pharaoh and his wife. He is seated, she is standing with her hand on his shoulder. The craftsmanship is outstanding. On the golden base of the second coffin, the goddess Isis is seen unfurling her wings protectively. There are hieroglyphics in the background which are meant as good wishes for the repose of the king. I found it hard to tear myself away from these beautiful things, but there were many other things to be seen.

We saw two painted limestone statues of Prince Rahotep and his beautiful wife Nofret - who was called 'the beautiful' (from the Old Kingdom). The tomb of Rahotep was located at Meydum, close to his father's pyramid, and the two limestone statues were placed inside it. The following morning we flew the short trip to Assuan where 'The Nile Star' was berthed. We would then proceed up the Nile. The vessel was air-conditioned and comfortable. Next day a felucca transported us to Elephantine Island where we saw the Botanical Gardens. We then drove to the granite quarries, after lunch on 'The Nile Star,' and saw an unfinished 137 foot obelisk. (The obelisk on the Embankment in London near the Houses of Parliament came from the same quarry). The 'sparkle' in the granite comes from specks of mica. I brought home a small piece.

The following morning we sailed at dawn to the sandstone hills of Genel Silsileh. On the west bank there are some 18th and 19th dynasty stelae (ancient upright stone tablets on which laws were carved) and a small chapel of the last king of the 18th dynasty, Horemheb (1334-1304 BC) he succeeded Tut-ankh-Amun.

Another short sail down the Nile to Edfu, where we took a horse-carriage to the Temple of Horus. We spent the night at El Kab. Breakfast over, we visited on foot Nekheb - the city of the vulture goddess Nekhbet. Then on to Luxor.

The following day - the day I had been waiting for - we crossed the Nile and drove to the Theban City of the Dead, where we visited the Valley of the Kings, carefully descending the slope to the tombs of Tut-ankh-Amun, Seti I, Ramesses VI. and Amenophia II, as well as the temple of Hatshepsut (although she was a Queen).

The name of Tut-ankh-Amun (1346-1334 BC) in the 18th dynasty, in the period known as the New Empire, must be one of the best known and maybe the best loved of all the Pharaohs. His tomb contained fabulous treasures and surprisingly was not discovered by grave robbers. There was sympathy also for the young King - and his Queen who died in tragic circumstances so soon after his death. One story says that he was killed during a hunt - whether by accident or design is not known. The law at that time was that if the young Queen wanted to take the throne, she must marry within twenty eight days after her husband's death. If no husband was found, she would have to relinquish the throne. It certainly looked very odd that two very young people should die so soon within a short time of each other. The person who eventually gained the throne was a government official named Horemheb. He was made king four years after the young Pharaoh's death. Ever since I could remember I had wanted to see his tomb, and was utterly thrilled to see the frescoes around the walls. The vivid colours looked fresh to me and I was amazed that they had been painted over three thousand years ago. Once again we saw the identical golden mask bearing his features on his coffin. I found it hard to tear myself away. It was terribly hot in the valley, dry and dusty, but bottled water was provided for our grateful party.

I had a very unnerving experience that day. It was whilst I was in the tomb of Ramses VI, there was only an elderly gentleman and myself in the tomb. The rest of the party were still behind. He seemed engrossed in a black stone about three feet high. I went over to look at it. It was then that a strange incident occurred. He placed his hands on the stone and immediately started shaking. He couldn't stop and looked very pale. I led him away, saying I would place my hands on the stone - which I did, but felt nothing- no reaction whatever. The gentleman looked as if he was going to pass out. By that time I wanted to get out as quickly as I could, but couldn't leave him there. To my relief the rest of the party had just entered the tomb so I explained what had occurred. They all in turn touched the black stone - nothing happened. We managed to get him outside into the sunshine where he looked all in. At the end of the day we once again boarded 'The Nile Star.' Cheryl gave him healing that night. He remained in his cabin for several days.

Ramses VI tomb was only a short distance from Tut-ankh-Amun's tomb. The young boy had succeeded his father-in-law Amenophis IV, but nowhere did we see Amenophis IV's tomb. He had so angered the people and priests of his day with his new cult on religion, that after his death his name had been erased from all monuments, temples etc. That meant that his tomb must have been destroyed. Tombs were constructed during the lifetime of a Pharaoh. If the black stone was connected with Amenophis IV it may have eventually found it's way into Ramses VI tomb (where the incident occurred). There certainly appeared to have been a great power attached to it - who knows what it had been connected with.

I was so glad I had taken Sally's book on Egyptian art as I was able to refer to it constantly. The rest of the party, like me, knew only a little of ancient Egypt, except for Cheryl, her husband and an Egyptian guide. Yes, it had been an interesting day, and if I had been overwhelmed by the Golden Mask of Tut-ankh-Amun, what must have been the feelings of the first Englishman, Howard Carter, when he discovered that breathtaking treasure, which was revealed to the world after it had lay buried for almost 3,000 years in the Egyptian desert!

The next day there was much talk. Was there a curse on the stone? Why was the old gentleman affected and no one else? Before retirement he had been an Anglican Minister. Also before the cruise he had visited a medium who informed him that way back in the time of the Pharaohs he had been a priest! And what was more interesting is that he hadn't been a good one. He may have been one of the priests opposed to Amenophis IV and his new religion.

After breakfast that day we visited El Amarna where Amenophis IV had lived on the Nile north of Thebes, which was then the capital. Little now remains of the city itself, but there has been excavation in the past fifty years which has revealed, apart from many works of art, the famous 'Armana Letters.' These are tablets referring to correspondence between the Pharaoh and Oriental courts.

The old gentleman was now much better, but did not go to El Amarna. He felt that his experience was a warning not to go. Strangely, a few other people didn't go either.

Only a few more days were left of our delightful and interesting tour. The weather was always in the nineties and even hotter, and for several days I felt jaded. I was sorry to miss 'The Valley of the Queens.' Eugenie also wasn't well with an ear infection, and she was confined to her cabin for a few days.

At dawn we sailed again. This time to Beni Suef, where we disembarked and drove to the 300 foot Meydum Pyramid, which was long thought to be built by Sneferu, some now believe it was the work of Huni, the last king of the 3rd dynasty, more than 4,600 years ago. That evening we sailed to El Ayat where 'The Nile Star' berthed for the night. We were instructed not to go ashore as there had been rumours there might be trouble. The following morning we heard thirty people had been killed. It wasn't until three weeks later - after we had arrived home - that we heard President Sadat had been murdered. Would this have had anything to do with the killings in El Ayat?

Two more days now remained of our cruise. We visited the famous Step Pyramid of Zoser at Sakkara - and before I had left for this

120

cruise, I had been asked by the healing circle which I attended in London if I could possibly bring back some sand - which is known for it's healing properties. So I wandered off by myself in search of some clean sand, away from the other tourists. The sand which has laid there for thousands of years is charged with energy from the sun and moon. Many healing circles now use this form of healing. As sand is heavy, I could only carry a small amount, and wondered how I was going to explain this to the Customs if I was searched.

We visited Memphis, the ancient capital of Lower Egypt, to see the colossal statue of Ramesses II and the alabaster Sphinx, then continued to Cairo where our evening was free. The next morning I was up early and packed presents and clothes, and after breakfast our coach took us to the airport. So ended a holiday of a lifetime.

Anthony was at the airport to meet me. He said I had grown thinner! He also said he had decided he wanted to become a pilot and would leave his job as a steward. He wanted to study and hoped to gain a commercial pilot's licence. He also wanted to see Australia.

Chapter Nineteen

CHANGES

There is a jewel which no Indian mine can buy
No chemic art can counterfeit;
It makes men rich in greatest poverty,
Makes water wine, turns wooden cups to gold
The homely whistle to sweet music's strain
Seldom it comes, to few from Heaven sent,
That much in little, - all in nought - content.

By an unknown author at the end of the XVI century.

I should have been content, but wasn't. The children by now were well into their careers, had left home, and visited me regularly, but the garden was much too large and needed all of my time, which I couldn't give as I attended lectures and other events regularly. Also, I did not need all the rooms now that they had left. So I decided to move, but where?

At our next circle meeting, Florrie said a message was coming through to me telling me to look for a Spiritualist church with a blue ceiling and pink walls, as this church would be the one I would eventually link up with.

"You might have to look over the border though, into another county," said Florrie.

Having had so much help and guidance from her in the past I did just this. First I obtained a list of all the churches in the county, and once a week made a visit, but nowhere were the walls pink or the ceiling blue. I was beginning to think Florrie was wrong. Then I found out that there was one place about forty miles away in the next county. So decided to visit it. I remember it was a bitterly cold night by the time I eventually arrived. I chose the night when a demonstration of clairvoyance was held. I entered the church and for the first five minutes didn't look up. I said to myself that if the walls were not as Florrie had predicted, then I wasn't going to look any further. Holding my breath I gazed up at the ceiling. To my joy I saw that it was pale blue and the walls were pink. So Florrie was correct again, I felt ashamed I had doubted her message. The first person I spoke to was the medium who ran the church. A very friendly and likeable person. So this would be the church I would be committed to. I arrived home late that evening, feeling much more contented than I had when I left earlier in the day. I was past the first hurdle. All I had to do now was to find a new house!

Then began the long and tedious job of finding a small bungalow near the church but within a reasonable distance from a railway station. Every week I was out visiting. Not only was I looking for a new place to live, but had the worry of selling my own house. Eventually I was lucky, as at the last minute everything seemed to go like clockwork. I was able to move in at the time it suited me. It was also my birthday, so I hoped it would be the beginning of a wonderful life, and being Easter also, there was the expectancy of spring flowers and new growth.

The church was luckily only eighteen miles from my bungalow, and a few minutes walk from the railway station. I joined the open circle and I attended regularly.

Roger still worked for the same firm who hired out holiday tents and mobile homes, but was now manager, continuing to visit France in the summer seeking out new sites. In May 1981, two days after his birthday, he married Faye whom he had met on a skiing holiday in Europe. It was their intention one day to own their own camping site. This they eventually did, buying a site in Brittany.

Louise was in her third year at college before finally obtaining her degree. Angela, now with three children, was quite content to continue nursing at her local hospital in the little village of Fairford, amidst the lovely countryside of Gloucestershire.

Anthony went to Australia later that year. He wrote regularly. In February 1982 we had a postcard saying, "Dear all, hope you're all well. Things are fine with me. Thanks for the long letter Mum.

Thanks again Lou for the lovely wine at Xmas. Mum, I listen to your tape in the car all the time (Ravel's Bolero). We have had the worst bush fires ever in Victoria, due to the very hot weather, drought and high winds. Thousands of hectares of bush in many areas have been destroyed, including hundreds of homes. Many have been left with nothing - only the clothes they were wearing. The community spirit is out of this world. Everybody helping in every way. Old age pensioners donating money. Relatives of friends of mine have been killed, also awful deaths of people incinerated by the 50 foot high, 3 km wide wall of flames. Thirteen firemen perished trying to hide under their fire truck from the heat - awful. I have another interview with Flight Service - keep yer fingers crossed. Love from Ant."

Yes, we all remembered the terrible pictures shown on TV that year, and naturally worried about him.

The following month when I again visited Dorothy's home circle Florrie said, "Your husband is so pleased the way the children have worked out their lives. 'Wish they would believe in this. Give them all my love. You are doing a lot of reading, and have learned a lot, now put it into practice.'"

Time went quickly by. Vivienne and I continued to write. She didn't go out much because of a bad heart. I kept her informed of unusual messages, and at a circle in the church, Doris, our secretary, noticed or 'saw' clairvoyantly a lady dressed in ancient Egyptian dress. She was holding out her arms, but Doris noticed she had no hands. This mystified Doris, who also held a development circle in her own house. It was there that one night one of the sitters went into trance, and the guide known as 'Red Eagle' came through her to inform Doris that far back in the time of the Ancient Egyptians, Doris had been the daughter of Nefertiti!! Doris was absolutely astonished at hearing this and more so when 'Red Eagle' told her that when she gave healing, Nefertiti was there to help her. The sitter, of course, was still in trance and new nothing of this, and was probably just as surprised as Doris on hearing this.

A week later I showed Doris my book on ancient Egyptian art and on one page there is a picture of Amenophis IV with his Queen, Nefertiti, holding hands in accordance with the widespread Amarnian practice of showing scenes of affectionate family life. Also a painted

125

limestone bust of the Head of Nefertiti showing the delicate and beautiful features of her eyes, pure profile and long neck. This can be seen in the Ehemals Staatliche Museen, Berlin. The limestone figures of Amenophis IV and his Queen can be seen at the Louvre Museum, Paris.

When I mentioned that they were holding hands, his right hand was holding her left hand. She had no right hand! As her husband Amenophis IV had turned the old religion upside down, and believed in One God (as did many of the cultured upper classes, where monotheism had long been practised) then they would have known and practised healing. This may have upset many of the lower classes and priests. Did they get their revenge on Amenophis IV by committing a cruel act on his beautiful Queen. She must have been a healer in her day, otherwise why should she come back and help Doris, and more to the point why should she 'appear' to Doris with no hands? There can be no doubt that Doris was once the daughter of Nefertiti. She could have helped the other healers in our church, but only comes through to Doris. The fact that this information came through a 'deceased' person (Red Eagle) is most remarkable.

Looking back it certainly seemed as if I was meant to visit Egypt. I would never have gone if I hadn't read that book on Egyptian art, which seemed to confirm what Doris had said about Nefertiti having no hands. Also, the incident in the tomb of Ramses VI, where the old gentleman was told, prior to the tour, that he had been a priest at the time of one of the Pharaohs.

I also became interested in the pendulum, and attended a demonstration at the Horticultural Halls in Victoria with Nellie. I used as my pendulum a tiny sea-horse covered with gold paint (given to me by Sally) attached to a gold thread. It proved very reliable, and gave accurate answers to questions put by my family. Especially as to unemployment, redundancies and travel etc., more on the pendulum in the next chapter.

Chapter Twenty

THE PENDULUM

The pendulum is an intermediary link with planetry vibrations. Each person has a vibratory link with what you call space, but in reality is the other world of the etheric. Each soul has a memory bank recorded in space; the past lives, this life so far lived, and future events for each individual are recorded. With the pendulum, one is able to make contact with the memory bank - either for oneself or for others.

When contacting the bank for others, it is wise to have the individual in front of one, or an object of that individual's before one, or better still in one's hand. Tune into that individual's vibrations by holding the pendulum over the being or object. When the pendulum has their measure, it automatically tunes in with their bank and if it is deemed advantageous the question will be answered.

Remember though, that when you ask a question involving another, that person's bank may not choose to answer. What may seem an ordinary question to the questioner, may be one which for the subject could cause repercussions if an answer pertaining to that person's present or future was given.

One must not abuse the pendulum, but use it wisely. It cannot answer falsely providing questions are put with honesty, without thought of personal gain and with the sole endeavour of improving one's own knowledge or aiding others. But remember you have a powerful instrument in your hands, if you ever use it wrongly, wrong answers can be obtained, for then you tune into influences which are not necessarily of a helpful nature.

Choice of Pendulum and its uses:
The pendulum itself should be well balanced of a clean or pure substance. Attention should also be given to the radio and/or television

waves, these can distort the vibrations of the pendulum if these instruments are on whilst the pendulum is being used. Similarly, electrical storms and other freaks of nature can distort the emanations over the ether.

As time goes by more and more people will come to recognise the potential of this instrument. It should not be used for foretelling the future in terms of fortune telling. It can be used to help direct one's pathway, spiritually, intellectually, and materially, where those physical things will be used to better one's spiritual self. Similarly, these same ideals can be used/applied on behalf of others.

The use of the pendulum for diagnosis of illness is of paramount importance. But a word of caution, do not rely solely on this means: use reason, listen to your innermost self, listen to your spirit doctors. The pendulum should work in harmony with all these things, not by itself.

You can use it to determine the colour rays which can help you or others to the betterment of each individual; to determine flowers, plants, herbs which can be used as medicines. To improve one's diet and ensure the body receives what it really needs.

It can help the soul with what it needs for peace, comfort and progress. By this we mean that the pendulum can direct you to music, the arts, hobbies and pursuits which are right for you.

The pendulum can be used for divining, but this is one of it's lowlier uses. Here we suggest that a hollow object is used which can be filled with the substance being divined. Take water for instance. An object of true metal or a wooden cask, preferably the latter can be filled; one of a large acorn size, or slightly larger is adequate.

Unlike the divining rod which must be taken over the actual area, the pendulum can be held over a map. The map should be a large one divided into sections so that the pendulum can swing freely over each section. When it gives a positive reading, enlarge this area and begin again. By a process of elimination the area in which to sink bores will be ascertained. Just think how much cheaper and quicker this method would be than those at present employed. A scientist sitting in his office perhaps, could divine water in Australia without the cost of setting up and kitting an expensive expedition.

Think too how much time could have been saved in your present quest for oil if a pendulum had been used. Coal mines, using coal, gold using a gold pendulum, and so on, could all be traced in this way. Just as individuals' have a memory bank so do nations. The pendulum can therefore be used to aid the prosperity of nations, to gauge the part one should play in one's nation, to analyse something of the karmic debt one's nation is paying.

Tests for the Pendulum:

You will want to apply the pendulum in many ways. Do remember that it is not a toy. It is a scientific instrument and should be used wisely, with forethought and an awareness of what you are doing for yourself and others by it's use. Do not neglect it's answers - put them into practise. If you don't you have wasted your time and energies in applying yourself to this study. Only with the right attitude of mind will you truly see the pendulum working correctly, with accuracy and foresight. As we have said already, the use of baser thoughts can conjure up baser answers. If you want to try some simple tests, make a chart of the week's weather, forecast the day ahead for set hours of the day and then compare with what eventuates. This will help you in compiling charts.

You can also try forecasting your health pattern for a month through positive and negative reactions. You must work out charts week by week, but the start of your individual week may not be the start of the calendar week. To begin, take each day of the week and get a reading. This will establish your day. From that map out each week on a sheet big enough to give you a sweep. Eventually you will establish those days which are your best; those your worst and those where you will have average vitality. From this you can plot your days to do strenuous things and those to ease up. This will also give you an idea of when you are most vulnerable to those minor illnesses to which you are susceptible. We emphasise that this chart cannot forecast any sudden disease you may develop.

The Pendulum in the Past:

The pendulum has been used for thousands of years. It was a common instrument in ancient China, and was used by medical men. The Greeks were also aware of it and used it for mental as well as physical ailments. The Chaldeans were aware of it, but the Egyptians were not followers of it to a great extent. Just as today methods come and go, so this was true of ancient times, and at the time of Egypt's known history, the pendulum was not popular.

If you study your ancient history, you will see that to a great extent the use of the pendulum rises and falls in keeping with the rise and fall of each Empire. For instance, as Egypt fell, Greece became dominant and so did the pendulum in their medicine.

The Renaissance in Europe brought forth the pendulum again, and the flood gates of the Aquarian Age which are now opening bring forth the pendulum once again. This time it's use will gradually become linked with science. It's use will move out of the shadows and thousands will come to know it's benefits.

Dictated by Spirit, September 1974
Susan Cover

Chapter Twenty One

SUPERSTITION - AND OMENS

Forsake the paths of ignorance and intolerance.
Be ye children of the Light. What do you fear?

Anon.

I always thought I was too modern to be superstitious, but at heart we are still primitive. Old wive's tales leave me cold, but in childhood I remembered once hearing that if a picture fell down a death was supposed to occur. So I was very worried when my wedding photograph crashed down near my head - in the middle of the night. I thought if a death did follow it may be uncle Bill who had a bad heart.

Later that day I was having a cup of tea and a chat with an old medium friend, when she suddenly said, "Do you know a Bill?"

"Yes, he is an uncle - why?" - I stopped speaking.

"Oh, nothing - they are just giving me the name Bill, that's all."

I explained that uncle Bill had been ill. If he had died, aunt Eva would have phoned me. That evening my brother had an uneasy feeling about uncle Bill. He phoned aunt Eva, (Bill's wife). Aunt Eva said uncle Bill was well, but thanks for ringing. The next morning aunt Eva phoned to say uncle Bill had died. I should not have been shocked as didn't I have a premonition, and yet I was upset, and a little bewildered. Were the spirit world trying to warn me I asked myself? I did not mention the message from my medium friend. This was not the time.

I tried to comfort my aunt on the phone. She was fifty miles away, I could not get there that day, but my brother would be seeing her, and would help her with the funeral arrangements.

We all met at my aunt's house on the day of the funeral which was chilly, but sunny. One can be so uplifted by the sun. Life must go on. The sun cheers and warms one even when one is low in spirits. One can even smile, it is such a wonderful tonic for tired nerves. How utterly devastating for funerals to be held on damp, foggy, dismal days, with the trees dripping rain, and one is shivering with the cold. One even thinks the deceased are well out of it!! My aunt was moved to tears when the Scouts and Scoutmaster lined up outside the chapel - all in uniform. Uncle Bill had been their Scoutmaster for years. Having no children, he had taken a fatherly interest in all his boys and was loved by all. Thirty wreaths had arrived from neighbours. Uncle Bill and aunt Eva had only been married for nine years. His second marriage, her first, (at the age of sixty!!). She had been friends with Uncle Bill's first wife. They had all met in church, where my aunt taught the Sunday School for forty years.

It was while driving back after the funeral that my mind was taken back to that day when I was having tea with my medium friend. I would love to tell my aunt, and was trying to sort the words out in my mind, when a golden opportunity presented itself. My aunt suddenly burst out and stunned me by saying, "If you're supposed to be a Spiritualist why weren't you told about Bill?"

I caught my breath, completely stunned by her remark. Quickly trying to regain my wits I wrestled with the idea of whether to tell her what I was told. Why shouldn't I tell her, it was the truth after all and she wanted the truth. I started from the beginning. She was very quiet, not interrupting me. At the end she said, looking at me directly, "How could they know about Bill when he wasn't even dead?"

Despite the occasion I nearly laughed. That was the sort of question a non-Spiritualist would ask, naturally enough.

"The same reason that they knew about my mother three weeks before she passed away. (My medium friend Florrie had said they were preparing a wreath for her. Florrie knew I was a Spiritualist, and that I would be upset about my mother, but not weighed down with grief as I had been with Stan). The spirit world try to prepare you in case there are any last minute things you want to tell them. In the case of family quarrels, how lovely to make peace before they are taken. "Do you remember I had made some cakes and had taken her lots of strawberries two days before she passed. I know spirit had reminded me, perhaps in my sleep. All I know is I felt I had to see mother - how upset I would have been if I had ignored those feelings," I said.

She digested this, and after a long pause said, "Well! I think it is wrong to look into the future, but if you do get a message from uncle Bill will you tell me?"

I couldn't believe my ears. Was this really my aunt speaking. A staunch Anglican, who thought all contact with the heavenly host was evil. She was now pleading with me to pass on a message if I received one.

"Of course I will," I said, completely overcome, "but you could have a message yourself if you went to a Spiritualist church, or a private sitting with a medium."

As soon as I said it I knew I had overstepped the mark. It was too soon. I should have taken it more slowly.

"I will never go to a medium," my aunt said, "or a Spiritualist church, but would like to know how Bill is."

"You're already half-way," I told myself, "why stop now?"

What is this fear which prevents people from wanting to know what lies beyond? It seemed to me as if she was having a battle with herself, whether to believe in her vicar's attack on Spiritualism, or to believe me who had had more than ample evidence.

"The spirit world is not there to put the fear of the Lord into us," I said. I then related all the messages I had received from various mediums. Some call the messages 'trivial' and so they are, except to the person concerned who desperately wants confirmation of the after-life. It is to that person alone that the message is given, no other. Would you say it is 'trivial' that a 'dead' person can talk to his wife through a medium? Everything in this world to me takes second place.

We were all ready for the buffet-lunch prepared by my aunt's neighbour, as most of us had travelled a long way that day. After a few hours, we thought it time to say farewell.

It was two weeks later that I received a phone call from Betty in Aylesford.

"Joyce, I'm sorry but I have some bad news - Dorothy died last night."

"Good God, that's the second," I muttered to my myself.

"Are you listening Joyce," Betty said anxiously.

"Yes Betty," I said.

We were both upset at losing Dorothy. How we would miss her afternoons which we had attended for several years.

"I had only visited her last week," I said.

"The funeral is next Monday - will you be going?" said Betty.

"Yes, will you be there?"

"No, I've made other plans, but will be with you in spirit," said Betty. She then told me how she had heard of Dorothy's death. Betty had been in the Spiritualist church that day. A picture (which Dorothy had given to the church) had fallen.

A friend of Dorothy's told the congregation that she had 'died' in hospital that day.

I arrived at the crematorium two hours before the funeral service, walking around the beautiful grounds, just thinking and meditating. It was the same crematorium where Stan was cremated. I had sworn I would never return to this place, a chilly breeze made me shiver and I was very glad when the funeral cars arrived. Then I met Florrie and other old friends. I was upset during the service not thinking of Dorothy so much as dear Stan. How I ever got through his funeral service I will never know, and afterwards talking to his old friend who had tears in his eyes. One can never forget these things, they are imprinted on our memory for all time.

We were invited to Dorothy's home for lunch. I had travelled over fifty miles by train to the funeral so was glad of the kind offer. It was so sad to see her chair empty, and I realised that never again would our circle be held in that home. It was the end of an era.

I was much too upset to read that evening, so settled myself in an armchair with one of Anthony's concoctions which he always brought back from 'The Duty Free' - I felt completely drained and wanted some drink to put some fresh life in me. Turning on the television and witnessing car crashes in a film, I quickly switched over to the news - another murder, a teenage girl this time. More grieving, more heartbreak for a family. It is these people Spiritualists are trying to help. To link them to the departed - who are just as desperate to get through. But how can they get through if no one is mediumistic in their family? They can only do so if one of the family contacts a medium. People who have this gift are either born with it or develop it when young, but many of our mediums were not encouraged to use their gifts, even though they were accurate in their predictions. This is a terrible shame, as those of us who wish to develop our psychic gifts have to sit in development circles for a number of years before the spirit world think us good enough to pass a message. It is not handed to anyone on a platter.

That evening I again lit the pink candle. The flame quivered at first then shot right up in the air. I knew Stan was with me and had been with me at the crematorium. I remembered his words to me through Florrie when he once said, "Don't go back to the crematorium, I am not there, but with you."

But of course I had to re-visit it for Dorothy's funeral. I also remembered the first time I had lit the candle when the beautiful rainbow appeared for a few minutes, then disappeared. I was told something would happen, and it did. They never fail to keep their promises. It is us who let them down.

It had been a long day. I was cold and miserable as I knew that I would never see again many of the friends in Dorothy's home circle. They had all travelled from various locations. Also, would Florrie want to continue her afternoons? Her journey took an hour and a half. The only person most suited to having a home circle was Anne, she lived only a mile from Dorothy's home, and her two teenage children were out at work during the day, so there would be no interruptions. If both Anne and Florrie agreed, we could still keep up the circle. I would go only once every three months instead of our fortnightly sessions, as the fare was very expensive and the journey too long. Dorothy's home had been a haven for me.

The following day I was sitting dejectedly when the telephone rang. It was an excited Betty.

"Joyce, what do you think - Dorothy has come through."

"Come through - where - how? I asked stupidly.

"I was in church today when a new medium visited us and gave an address. She said a Dorothy White was here, was feeling tired but would come through later. It was wonderful Joyce, I wish you could have been here." Betty sounded jubilant.

"That's fantastic," I said. Of course Dorothy would come back to the church. It was her church. She had started it, polished, decorated, and cleaned it. Despite this I never thought she could have come back so quickly.

"What a pity her family couldn't have been in the church when the message was given," I said.

Dorothy's family were Catholics who deny all thoughts of communion - spiritual communion that is - and yet according to their faith the Virgin Mary appeared to children and many people in Medjugorje in Yugoslavia quite recently. The holy apparition first appeared in 1981 to six children. Was she trying to warn the people of some impending disaster which would befall the country? The priests banned people from going in the end, saying it was becoming a tourist attraction, of course it was, and what was wrong in that. Isn't Lourdes such a place?

For a time the apparition only appeared to the children. They said it was a beautiful woman, and thought it was the Virgin Mary. She gave them messages. Later she appeared in the village church each evening. Many people saw her and heard her. They were told to pray and fast. The Bishop of the diocese was informed, and it was his idea that tourists were discouraged. There was no doubt she was trying to tell the people something. Once again the priests had to interfere. The messages were sincere, and if followed carefully would have averted the terrible tragedy which was to befall the country later. Why is it that the Church think that every message coming from the spirit world is evil? Once again they read their Bible but do not understand it. All priests in the future should have knowledge of all religions. One is no greater than the rest. Strangely all believe in another world - their religions teach them that. But Christianity alone says one must not attempt to reach this world. All the dark skinned races believe in this very strongly, and have their own healing services and seances. Their mediums are excellent. One white woman in South Africa whilst I was there always visited the local Witch Doctor for advice. She said he was always true, and recommended herbs for her ailments. White doctors could learn a lot from them.

On hearing I was now a member of the Spiritualist church, one person remarked, "Twixt two stools you'll fall."

Was that remark supposed to represent Good and Evil? If so, which was the good Church and which the Evil? Don't tell me, let me guess!! If I had fallen on the 'Good' side then I would never have written this book, and my knowledge of the next world would be nil. Because however I fell on the 'Bad' side I am more knowledgeable, more tolerant of people's behaviour, and have no fear of death, and know that each little effort on our part brings its own reward. Not only to ourselves, but to others. It is said in the Bible, "You cannot serve two masters, God and Mammon." You also cannot serve good and evil. If you do faithfully what you know to be best, then you are serving man. I believe that is the second commandment, and one which is the most important in the eyes of the Spiritualist. God and one's neighbour must come under the same heading - if they are served with love, which is the embodiment of every good thing. Is it any wonder then that I left the Anglican Church when an Anglican vicar, a young vicar too, told me that the Spiritualist Church was evil, full of evil spirits.(I wonder if secretly he knew our congregations were larger than his).

Also he was paid for his Sunday sermons. Our mediums weren't, or for the hours our healers put in, not only on Sundays, but weekdays. A healer would be pretty tired or ill before he refused to see anyone.

Chapter Twenty Two

HAPPIER TIMES

Towards the dawning of another year we journey on.
Troubles lose their blackness when faced with courage and a smile.

By John Wesley.

The year 1983 was a good one. I had a lovely holiday in France with Angela, Richard and the children. We stayed at one of Roger's firm's campsites, in a mobile home. Louise and Patrick joined us. Louise was doing some photography for a brochure for Roger's firm. We had sun every day and swimming was a delight. A perfect crossing home on the 6 o'clock ferry, not a ripple on the sea. The only thing which marred it was when we arrived at Angela's home to find there had been a power cut and all the frozen food in the freezer was limp and soggy.

That September Eugenie and I saw Boridin's 'Prince Igor' at the Albert Hall with full choir. A wonderful performance. We went on the off chance not knowing what was being played that evening. I had first heard it when Stan played it to me on his gramophone. It was a great favourite of mine and I was overjoyed when we booked the seats. It was played to a packed hall. I only go once a year, twice if possible, so am sure Stan had impressed me to go knowing how much I liked Borodin's music.

It was now November, and I was just thinking of sending Anthony a present in Australia for Christmas, when the following morning I received a postcard from him. It was of Westgate Bridge, Melbourne. The postcard read, "Dear Mum, just a quicky to tell you I'm still alive and kicking. I'm now settling into my new home. My commercial pilot written exams are next week, and are extremely difficult. I have been studying hard for them these last few weeks. I passed my P.P.L. flight test two weeks ago (the next licence up from a private). I'm now allowed to fly a twin-engine A/C as well in Aussie. I went flying the other day and took a video tape of this exact spot by air (the view on the postcard). I will send the tape to you for Christmas. Keep this card and compare the sights - of course the video film is very bumpy-due to turbulence. Sally is coming out here next week. We're both very excited about our holiday, and to be seeing each other again. Bye for now, Love Ant. Love to all."

Two weeks before Christmas I received Adelaide's Christmas card. (We had been writing since 1960) and also Joan's card from Canada. (We had been corresponding since we were fourteen years of age). Joan was hoping to visit her sister Audrey in Norway the following summer, and time permitting would come to the UK. During the war Audrey had met a handsome Norwegian sailor, and we would all go dancing, Joan, Audrey and I with Gustav and his friends.

I hadn't written to Vivienne for a long time and felt very guilty. Life seemed so hectic now. I still attended weekly lectures in London with friends and went on several National Federation of Spiritual Healers courses. Also a course on 'Awareness' at the College of Psychic Studies. The College had also arranged a course on the lovely island of Iona for a week, twenty of us attended. It was in May and very chilly. I decided to go on the shuttle, a one hour trip to Glasgow from Heathrow, and wished I hadn't as it was bedlam due to the noisy Scots football enthusiasts shouting at each other, the stewardess desperately trying to make herself heard, in getting them to fix their safety belts!! By the time they had all obeyed this instruction it was time to get off. Once at Glasgow, I caught the four hour train to Oban. It was a pleasant journey after the last one. We stopped at a station where we alighted and had tea and scones, and then continued our journey.

I arrived at Oban at 5 o'clock in the evening, only to find I had missed the last ferry to the Isle of Mull, so had to put up at a guest house near the harbour. So far I hadn't met any other person on the course in Iona. The next morning I arrived in time to catch the 10 o'clock ferry. A warm day, but breezy. From the Isle of Mull it was a short trip to Iona. The hotel was welcoming and people gradually drifted in, and a few came from Rhodesia, the whites still called it that I noticed. It must be hard to call ones country by another name when one has lived there for years. We all wanted to see the Abbey, and were shown around whilst the history of the place was explained.

Our hotel was named after the great Saint Columba who first landed on the south of the island now called Columba's bay.

Lectures were held in the mornings. One day a small group decided to visit the famous Fingal's Cave on the Isle of Staffa, about eight miles north of Iona. We had to go when the weather was suitable by boat, and not too rough. I asked several people why it was called 'Fingal's Cave' - nobody knew.

It really is a most striking and bizarre neatly arranged column of rocks- like organ pipes - from a distance. I have never seen anything like it. It said in my Observer's book of geology that of all the geological formations, surely the most striking is the columnar structure of Fingal's Cave in the Island of Iona, and the Giant's Causeway on the coast of Northern Ireland. The rock in these regions is basalt. The cave itself was dark and eerie, the day was cloudy and when the waves buffeted against the rocks it wasn't exactly a pleasant place to be. When Mendelssohn visited it, the day must have been beautiful and sunny, with calm sea, otherwise he couldn't possibly have composed such beautiful music. It had been an interesting day, made more so by my seeing for the first time a double rainbow - over the Isle of Mull. The folk on the Island of Iona say they often have clear skies when there are clouds over the Isle of Mull.

The short course ended. After the boat trip to Oban I was given a lift to Glasgow where once again I caught the shuttle to Heathrow. Here I waited for a Green-line coach to our nearest railway station where Roger had arranged to meet me. I waited an hour. It was 11 o'clock in the evening. I could barely see someone gradually approaching in the darkness. It was Roger limping. The car had broken down and he had had to walk about four miles, through country lanes. We couldn't get a taxi so had to walk home. Roger looked all in. I think that was the longest day of my life as I had travelled by boat, car, plane and coach and then a four mile walk at the end!!

Chapter Twenty Three

HEALING IN THE BEYOND

Life, full of vigour and progressive thought, and the passing on to a higher Sphere. All beauty and full perfection, no decay, no death. Shake from your shoulders that dark mantle, and behold the more beautiful one which shall be yours.

By John Keble.

These few pages were written by Harriet McIndoe in the magazine "Two Worlds" dated January 1980, and tells of a trance medium named Edith Thomson, and one of her guides called Silver Pine, a healer. In trance one day Silver Pine came through with this message: *"Most people think that when their friends are 'dead' they immediately become happy and well. The majority of people, however, have to make many adjustments before they find real happiness. Health and happiness with us are synonymous.*

You have heard of healing places in the Spirit World, hospitals as you would say. I have in my care such a place, where I gather those skilled in the art of re-adjustment. Some people are naturally skilled in this work, but must have to be trained very carefully for it.

Many young men and women gladly surrender themselves to the work of healing. 'I desire to serve' they say. No one is refused the chance to learn what such service involves. There are many tests they must pass, without knowing they are tests. They must have endurance, sympathy, love, truth, foresight, and a sense of humour. They must be compassionate, though just, and, above all things, they must have that resilience of spirit which never can be bowed down.

Very few pass these tests immediately, so training must be undergone by those who desire to work in our centre. They must themselves be readjusted. The first principle is renunciation. They start naked, stripped of all preconceived ideas of their own worth. The pure soul stands ready to acquire and learn anew. As they progress they become naturally joyous, buoyant spirits of whom you might think that they were perhaps rather childish, if you came upon them in their leisure hours and observed their laughter and joy in one another. They have learned true happiness, expressive happiness. They are not dulled, nor do they take on the ornament of a great profession. They have simple clothing, a uniformity, so that their blending together is not disturbed by too much individualism, though each must be an individualist.

Each helper must understand the basic principles underlying health, and I do not speak here of physical health. They must study psychology. They must understand why the self desires certain things, and the responses to stimuli and colour. Such understanding is acquired only gradually.

You may be imagining a large institution with beds, doctors and nurses. Such is not the case. My particular theory is that reconstruction, to be effective, must be begun on the right lines, so I never permit the carrying over of an illusion, or a desire on the patient's part to hold fast to a state of invalidism. Our methods are quite different from yours, although even among you there are some clinics where adjustments are made through surroundings. Colour and natural influences help the individual to adjust to the normal. The conditions of restoration are available on earth as in the spirit. They depend entirely on the individual patient. That is why an understanding of psychology is so necessary.

A helper is of little value if he cannot analyse the condition of the patient by glance, by contact, and through talking with him, and so decide the attention that is needed. We know that only certain people can help certain others, so that the person best fitted to give help, is drawn to the one who needs it.

Some people are brought to our notice before their deaths by friends, either on earth or in the spirit world, who apply to us for help. We prefer to link with people before death to give us power to bring them under our influence, so that they wake into surroundings already prepared. Colour, breezes, and spiritual influence play upon them

144

and bring about once more the desire to live, and to live in health. That such preparations are necessary is to many people a shock, because of the old idea of transformation on death, but the only transformation is brought about by gradual change.

Some people are malformed mentally from birth and this is difficult to eradicate. Some are the innocent victims of environment and heredity; others of their own self-indulgence. Many come from the scrapheaps of humanity, waifs and strays with no abiding place even on earth, although some may have the seeming covering of respectability.

Many people adjust themselves to their new life very quickly. Mentally bright people are the quickest to respond. Those who are suspicious, even of the conditions into which we put so much love, are very difficult to help. When faced with love they become afraid of themselves, as well as those who shower it on them. Many people are afraid to enter the conditions which would bring out the best in them, and so they live an abnormal life.

I wish you could come with me to the various places we have. In some, insane people are treated. I am not speaking of imbeciles at present. We induce a state of complete passivity. This is necessary so that we can begin the process of re-education from the start. A deep sleep, or trance state, supervenes. It is not hypnotic. There is a gradual awakening.

Then there is a series of small glass-like houses where, in a partly conscious state, the mind is learning to be alone with itself. Farther on you would see the attendants speaking to the patients and making suggestions. Later you would see him walking in the gardens, doing a little easy work, being attended by companions who give the service naturally given to a little child.

On earth doctors must certify a person as insane and then he is bundled away into an institution. In the Spirit World relatives of a new arrival often have some such difficulties to deal with, but the problem is not necessarily insanity as it is known on earth. Many things give alarm in spirit which are not even considered eccentric on earth.

The family is an integral part of man's relationships and the family still holds good here. When people arrive they make union again with

145

their relatives. In some instances these relatives may find difficulties arising. The strange behaviour of a newcomer may startle them. They will talk one with another, saying, 'What can be done?' They will approach an elder among them and ask him to speak to the recalcitrant one, who resents that. He thinks them old-fashioned. After all, they've been a long time dead.

Sometimes the family asks us to help. We try to persuade the newcomer that there is something a little wrong. By psychological methods we get him to accept our ministrations for a period.

We gather together those who really are mentally ill; those with brains undeveloped since childhood; those who are eccentric, like misers; and those who are very important. Even ordinary people find it very difficult to get into the smallness of the real self.

Most of these have to be willing patients. Nothing is applied that would make them feel uncomfortable. Even the most important people are treated as they feel they should be treated. We all go round being very important together. We mix people carefully, so that like meets like. Important people have to deal with important people, so that the meek and mild are not imposed upon. It's all so natural that the individual doesn't realise what has happened. He's often not aware that he's receiving any special treatment.

There are people who have hoarded money, left it hidden somewhere, been suspicious of banks and neighbours, gone in rags, picked up cigarette ends. They do the same things here, but find it difficult to pick up cigarette ends. They are afraid to wear nice clothes in case people think they have money.

These misers are in a doleful state if they have no money, so we manufacture money. By making conditions alike for all of them, we take away competition. The miser gradually realises there is no need to be afraid, but he is still suspicious, and hides his money from his neighbours. As adjustment begins free access is made possible to all that he needs, and there is no longer any incentive to keep on hoarding.

The miracle begins when he wants to give something away. At first he does not give, but furtively puts things away from him. Then he actually gives something away, but finds that the recipient has no use for it. It is not really a gift, for it is something he does not want and

*is trying to get rid of. We try to woo him from self-centredness by
surrounding him with things that he covets.*

*By beauty, love and laughter we wake him to the knowledge that the
world is a very beautiful place, and that the eye must look outwards
to perceive beauty; that possessions as such mean nothing; that true
satisfaction comes from understanding spiritual things; and that no
virtue accrues from giving, but the sheer joy of sharing with another.
When an individual possesses nothing and is ready to go out to give
and to create, he is cured.*

*I have been told that there is an idea abroad that in the spirit world
there are large institutions or hospitals where Sisters of Mercy bring
people from lower regions, from hell. This probably comes from
attempts to translate ideas into words. It is difficult to give you the
picture as it is. It probably came through mediums by mental impact,
which is not close enough for true translation.*

*People who eschew trance and control know very little of the fineness
necessary to be in rapport with refined spirits. The interpretation of
the thought impulse is therefore couched by the medium in his own
language and ideas.*

*I'd like to paint a brighter picture, of sunny vales and hills and grassy
places; of trees and flowers and children, of love and companionship;
and of attendants who do not wear the garb of solemnity, but adopt
the role most suited to the environment of the patients."*

Thus ends this vital message given by Silver Pine.

Among those he treats as a healer are many recently dead who find
it difficult to adjust to their new environment. Knowing the wonderful
life in store then, wouldn't people want to know this knowledge;
would insist on all churches teaching them this knowledge. Have you
learned anything from this book? Then it has been well worthwhile.
Do you agree that bereaved people would benefit from this
knowledge? And is there any reason why they should not do so? And
do you think it is wicked to 'contact the dead' considering that some
of them are your own relatives!! Do you often think of them
nostalgically at Christmas, longing to relive old times? Well all that
is possible. But if most churches get their way, our churches would
be closed down. Would you like to know more of this 'other' life?
Then do so for yourself. I have told you of the places which have

helped me. They are certainly not 'resting in peace' as my vicar once told me. In fact most of the vicars are the worst type of teacher to talk of the 'other' life considering they have not spoken to the 'departed.' Each must find out for himself.

Buddha once said:-

Believe nothing because someone else believes it.
Believe nothing because a belief is generally held.
Believe nothing because a so-called wise man said it.
Believe nothing because it is written in sacred books.
Believe nothing because it is said to be of divine origin.
Believe when the written document or saying is corroborated by your own reason and consciousness.

You therefore do not have to believe my story, except that it is the truth. I certainly gain nothing by telling an untruth, but everything by telling the truth. Wouldn't every person like to know what is going to happen to his soul? Or whether he will meet again his 'twin-soul'? If you don't love anyone in this world, then it won't matter one way or the other to you, but there may be someone in the spirit world who loves you, and is anxiously awaiting that reunion.

Chapter Twenty Four

TRUE FRIENDSHIP

True friendship is one of God's greatest gifts.
True friendship is of God, and belongs to Spirit - is Divine

By John Wesley.

That day I was to make a new friend. It was a Sunday. As I passed our local newspaper shop I bumped into a lady emerging from it. One glance told me she was much distressed. I asked if I could help. She was crying and couldn't speak for a while. She eventually said she had just moved into the district and didn't know a soul. I said my house was only a few yards away and would she like to come in, she accepted thankfully.

It was a cold day so I gave her some ginger wine. After a while she told me her husband had died only a week ago, she had gone to her local church but received no comfort. It was a double tragedy for her, to move is a traumatic time - in addition, to lose a husband after just moving into a new home, and giving up one's friends and familiar places must have made it a terrible time for her.

Naturally, after she had talked I spoke of my bereavement, and how I had coped. She seemed very interested, so I gave her some books which I thought might be of interest to her. One was entitled 'What is Spiritualism' the other was 'A Venture in Immortality' by David Kennedy, a Minister in the Church of Scotland. Also a few 'Two Worlds' magazines which I received each month, now in it's 109th year. It features Spiritualism and the paranormal.

Two weeks later she returned with the books. I tentatively asked if she would like to visit the Spiritualists Association of Great Britain and have a sitting with a medium. She agreed, so I gave her the monthly magazine, listing mediums and the dates they would be giving their demonstrations. She was therefore able to choose her own time and medium of her choice. I told her to take a pen and pencil as she couldn't possibly remember everything they said, especially if she had an hour's sitting. I asked her if she would please come back and let me know what she thought of it.

She was back two days later. By sheer coincidence she had booked with a medium who came from her own town up north. The demonstration was wonderful she said. First he told her that a man was with her and that a dog was with him. The dog had died on his lap. She gasped at this, as her dog had died on her husband's lap before they moved into the new house. Other pieces of news were given about her family which she readily understood. I asked her how the family had reacted to this. She replied that they had said if it cheered her up then that was alright. Cheer is hardly the word I would have used, but at least they didn't put obstacles in her way.

I also valued the friendship between Anne and Betty whom I tried to see whenever possible. Nellie I continued to see at lectures. These widened our horizons, one subject leading to another, and meeting new people.

It was now April 1985 and on my birthday I received a card from Anthony, with an aerial view overlooking the Macintyre River and Inverell, New South Wales. It read, "Hi, Ma, I've been very busy this last month with charter and joy flights over 12,000 dollars cash over the Easter hols. Thousands of tourists came and passed thru Lightning Ridge. Am just doing a charter flt., to Inverell, N.S.W. - a pretty place. Many rich people and houses here, so it's another good place to do aerial photography, plus it's got great potential to start a charter Coy, have food for thought. Hope you had a nice birthday. The temp: here is still boiling hot and humid. I had to fly around a few thunder storms to get here - quite turbulent. My love to all the family. Love from Ant."

Anne, Florrie and I agreed to hold a three monthly meeting at Anne's home, and it was at the following meeting that Florrie surprised me by telling me that Anthony would soon be home. I had Anthony's postcard with me so read it to them. Nothing about coming home.

"Oh well, but I think you will find he will be home for next Christmas

150

and you'll all have a wonderful time. Your husband is saying, 'Give them all my love and take care of yourself.'"

As all my messages were on tape it meant carrying my recorder around, it was very heavy. It usually took me about four hours by train from Anne's to my home, changing three times, so it was a long day.

The garden was beginning to look quite pretty with spring bulbs everywhere. If Anthony arrived home at Christmas, there wouldn't be anything in the garden. Still, I didn't expect he would even notice. We would probably spend the Christmas with my daughter Angela in her cottage in the little village in Fairford. Gloucestershire is a pretty county in the Cotswolds. Fields are generally separated by walls, not hedges, as in my county, and most of the cottages and houses are built of local grey stone which gives a clean look about the place and blends in nicely with all the summer flowers and plants. This gives an added interest when travelling. I like the people also. They have the time to speak and give strangers the idea they are not going to hurry for anyone. This is in the country of course. The towns are just like any other town. Cars and noise.

My new friend called regularly. Each time I lent her more books. Two she found helpful were 'Excursions to the Spirit World' and 'More about the Spirit World' by Frederick C. Sculthorpe. I had collected by now a variety of books, lent many, but did not get them all back. As books are now expensive I have stopped this but tell folk where they can buy them. I naturally hope my own children will read them one day.

Patrick's father recommended I read 'The Awakening Letters.' I bought five books from the College of Psychic Studies. One for myself and one for each of the children. I don't think they ever got past the first page! The book was written by Lady Sandys and Rosamund Lehmann, whose daughters both died young in tragic circumstances. A very good account of life in spirit from people from all backgrounds. A chapter is devoted to healing from spirit. There is no need for anyone to be ignorant of this subject.

It was in the following October that I heard that Anthony would be coming home, and on the 27th November received his last postcard with an aerial view of Sydney Opera House. It read, "Dear Mum and

all, having all sorts of problems getting away. Two pilots have let me down. One because he was incompetent. The other because at the last moment he decided he didn't like Lightning Ridge. Another chap I had on standby, as a last resort, failed his Chief Pilot's interview (inadequate experience) so I had to postpone my flight to Los Angeles. However I hope to leave this weekend IF I can get a seat as they are all booked. (I've now managed to get another chap). I will let you know if I cannot make our previous date. So, if you don't hear from me you'll know I've got on, OK? I'll see you on the 7th December on Flight TE006 at London Gatwick. I'm absolutely exhausted now, as I've been flying backwards and forwards from Sydney interviewing pilots and doing all those last minute things that inevitably crop up and have to be done. See ya soon, Love Ant."
So Florrie was right again as she said months ago that Anthony would be coming home at Christmas!

Chapter Twenty Five

WEDDING BELLS

Misses! the tale I relate
This lesson seems to carry -
Choose not alone a proper mate,
But proper time to marry.

By Cowper.

Our youngest at last decided to marry. As Louise and Patrick had been good friends for quite a few years, I thought the proper time had now come for them to marry. Florrie had told me four years before that there would be a wedding in the month of May. It would be a lovely affair, and would I please wear pink as Stan liked me in that colour? They wished to marry on Louise's birthday 2nd May, but the vicar couldn't arrange it then but if they could bring the date forward three days it could be arranged. So it was settled. This proves to me how our idea of time differs from the spirit world. When Florrie told me there would be a wedding in May, I naturally assumed it would be the following May, but no, I was wrong, and four years were to pass before they eventually married. The spirit world knew they wanted to marry in May but it had to be changed because of events not of their making on 29th April.

Louise's dress was perfect and fitted her beautifully with a pretty bow at the back, laced with pink ribbons, and the same ribbons on the sleeves to match the pink of the roses in her bouquet- and coronet. I wished Stan could have been there, but I know he was in spirit. It was left to Roger to give her away which he did, playing the part well, and delivering a humorous speech during the reception.

My dress it seemed was arranged by the spirit world. Stan wanted me in pink, so I visited a London store and bought a pink chiffon dress, very pretty and ideal for a wedding. When I arrived home, and told Louise that they also had it in blue, she said she would have liked me in blue. I thought after all it was her wedding and she should have a say in it so went back to the store, and reluctantly bought the blue dress. I arrived home and Louise asked me to try it on. She looked at my face and said, "You'd much rather have the pink dress wouldn't you?"

"Yes," I said.

"Well go back to the shop and explain," she said.

"Suppose it has already been sold?"

"Well, they have the same shop in Guildford. I will go there and see if they have a pink dress like yours in the same size."

Meanwhile I went back to the shop, feeling very foolish as this was the third time I had been. The assistant was very understanding, it was a wedding after all.

I asked if I could borrow their telephone book, and phoned the same store in Guildford. I explained to an assistant that a young lady would be there that afternoon looking for a dress, and gave her the colour and size, but to tell her not to bother, as I had bought the dress in London. Louise phoned the London shop to ask if the one remaining pink dress in my size was still there. She was disappointed to hear that the dress had already been sold. You can imagine her surprise when she rang me later to find that it was I who had bought the pink dress! Luckily it was still there. It really was a stroke of luck as it was in a sale and others had looked at it. Stan had had his way after all!

Louise's in-laws I had met only once. Patrick's father as mentioned before was a spiritual healer at 'The White Eagle Lodge' in Liss. Strangely they did not have messages from a medium on the platform like we did in our churches. This may have changed now, I do not know as I have never been there. If they do not, it is astonishing when it was Grace Cooke (through her guide White Eagle) who made the White Eagle Lodge possible. It was also Grace who was the medium contacted by Sir Arthur Conan Doyle after his passing. (Patrick's family are distantly related to Grace by marriage). Conan Doyle had spent half his life bringing Spiritualism to the masses and travelled extensively, teaching Spiritualism. Thousands had gathered at The

Albert Hall, in London, for the memorial service, held a few days after his passing, in 1930. Pictures in glass frames of all the famous pioneers of Spiritualism can be seen in one of the upper rooms at the Spiritualist Association of Great Britain. Conan Doyle of course is there. I hope there is a picture of him at The White Eagle Lodge.

In his book, 'The Wanderings of a Spiritualist,' Conan Doyle wrote, "To give religion a foundation of rock instead of quicksand, to remove the legitimate doubts of earnest minds, to make the invisible forces with their moral reactions a real thing, and to reassure the human race as to the future which awaits it - surely no more glorious message was ever heralded to mankind."

There only remained now for Anthony to marry. Both he and Sally had managed to come to Louise's wedding with little rest from their long flights from the day before. Many stewardesses were off sick during long flights and Sally often caught colds and flue like symptoms. Anthony had been lucky and now worked for Virgin Airlines under their charismatic boss Richard Branson. It was an excellent airline and Anthony was happy. His flights included America, Tokyo and Moscow. The latter took four hours. One day after a trip to Moscow he phoned me, and was much amused when I told him I had that day visited a friend in Maidstone Kent, a journey of not more than fifty miles, it entailed changing at Gatwick, Redhill, Tonbridge, Paddock Wood and Maidstone - time taken four hours! By British Rail of course.

Chapter Twenty Six

REFLECTIONS

To contemplate the future with calmness and serenity,
You have begun to learn the steps which lead ever upwards.
You have found interest in the wonders opening out before
your eyes.
You have cleared your mind of the dust of ages.
New thoughts come crowding in.
The study is deep, absorbing and full of interest
for those who investigate slowly and carefully.

By Manuel.

And so I almost reach the end and briefly remind you of the events which convinced me of the higher life.

First the message from Stan insisting his watch was for me. The compensation I should receive. The description by the medium of Stan's accident prior to my attending his inquest. His 'thankyou' for the flowers I placed on my dressing table, with the name and amount of the flowers. The orange geum which suddenly appeared in my garden on the anniversary of my mother's death. Plus the urgent message from Stan at the exact time of her death.

As nature re-awakes each spring, why should mere man be neglected? Our spring is in the spirit world. Each can be given spiritual sight if he will banish fear - fear of the unknown. Should you have similar experiences please pass them on, someone with similar psychic accounts may only be too willing to discuss them with you. I have found one is always 'led' to those who need help. Spiritualism is now coming out into the open through lectures, films and debates, and there are several places in London and in the home counties where

157

one can learn all about the mechanics of mediumship. It is essential one goes to the right place, which is NOT the Ouija board! It is also very upsetting how many people confuse Spiritualism with the Ouija. One is spiritual, the other isn't. I have attended hundreds of seances with first class mediums, and never has a Ouija board been used.

To those who cannot believe a person can communicate with a loved one who is in the spirit world, these will find it doubly difficult to believe that an animal can also communicate, but this was confirmed to me after my son's Alsatian dog was 'seen' by a clairvoyant running towards me. He said it was a beautiful dog, beautiful in nature he meant, a very spiritual dog. I had loved that dog, so why shouldn't he come back to me. My son Roger was deeply upset when it died. So I bought him and Faye a book entitled 'When Your Animal Dies' by Sylvia Barbanell, a great comfort to anyone who has lost a beloved animal. As well as man, an animal also takes it's memory with them, as your home was his home.

Three weeks later Roger's other dog - a mastiff - also died. I think from a broken heart - although there was also something wrong with it. The two dogs were inseparable, and of course they still are. Animals fill a need in our lives which nothing else can replace.

My clock stopped for three days after the dog died. It was battery run. After the third day the clock started again on it's own. The battery was still working. As mentioned earlier in the book, our family clock also stopped at the exact moment of my father's death - at three o'clock in the afternoon. It was undoubtedly stopped by a spirit hand to make us aware and to investigate psychic phenomena for ourselves. To realise just how close the spirit world is to us. Also, just prior to auntie Eva's husband's death, my wedding photo crashed to the ground.

Why are so many people reluctant to call on a bereaved person? They will call in sickness, yet to the bereaved it is far worse than any illness. Do they really think that by not talking about the deceased they are doing the one left behind a favour? The bereaved person desperately trying to control their feelings, and the caller wishing they could leave as quickly as possible. So both are playing a part. A wasted call, as neither benefited. The bereaved want to talk. They are trying to give you a picture of what they have been through. A friend in need is a friend indeed, you don't have to talk, just listen. This is where a small group of people in similar circumstances can really help each other. I was fortunate in meeting a group of Spiritualists. I could have never survived without them. As for my Christian 'friends,' I could have never survived with them!

The spirits also have a humorous side to their natures as I was to find out one evening. I arrived home late, had a quick meal and a bath, and just before going to bed dropped my ring on the carpet. I made a hasty half-hearted search but couldn't find it, as it was very late I decided to leave it, I knew where it was after all and I was very tired. The following morning after breakfast I remembered it, and again looked for it. It was not on the carpet. I emptied out shoes and slippers. I stripped the bed of blankets. I threw everything out of the room and hoovered it thoroughly, then inspected the hoover. I even looked into trinket boxes, although I knew it had fallen on the floor. I was scared by this time, for it was my mother's ring and a solitaire diamond. It was given to her by my father, and was quite expensive. I had wall to wall carpeting, so it couldn't have slipped through to the floorboards. It was a mystery. I searched again. In desperation I sat down and picked up a pen and paper and wrote a short note to my mother. After all it was her ring! The note was short and to the point, "Dear mother, I have lost your ring, please help me find it. Love from Joyce."

Feeling a bit silly I propped it against a vase of flowers which I always have in my bedroom for Stan.

I decided to get on with the rest of my housework as two hours had been taken up with the searching. Every now and then I went in, not knowing what I would see, but hoping the ring had been found. The day went quickly, as I had a large garden to look after. That evening at nine o'clock I was listening to the news on the television. Whilst listening I was pinning up my hair searching for hairpins in the small trinket box, when I heard a click, and to my utter astonishment I saw the ring in the box. It was not there before as I had looked into every vase and box in my bedroom, not once but many times. There was no doubt in my mind that someone had dropped it in. Why had they taken it in the first place? Was it to show me that there was nothing they couldn't do? This is what is known as an 'apport.' Gordon

Higginson at Stansted Hall once gave a demonstration at a psychic phenomena weekend on 'apports' and we all saw a rose suddenly materialise. The rose was handed around and we all saw and felt it, still wet with dew. A flower called a Hosta also materialised, and Gordon said that a man in the spirit world is handing it to a lady in the room who wanted a cutting of it from his garden, and had asked for it many times but he always forgot, now he remembers. He is giving it to her with his love.

The next time we met in Florrie's circle I mentioned the incident. She was quiet for a while, then said, "Your mother is laughing - she is saying there are fairies at the bottom of your garden."

Well, as I cannot see them I cannot argue with that statement. My garden had a circle of mushrooms which looked very ethereal on a moonlight night. Whilst on a weekend course at Stansted Hall later, the room was packed, yet the medium pointed at me and said, "I can see fairies all around you, have you been reading about them?"

I did buy a book, with beautiful coloured pictures of elves and fairies with an article on every page, which told of people who had actually seen them and where they had seen them. They are known as 'elementals.' There are spirits in the whole of nature. In water, in plants, in trees. Each have a particular job to do. It seems our childrens' books of long ago contained a lot of truth.

I was paid a great compliment one day when at a demonstration given by Ivy Northage at the Spiritualists Association of Great Britain. She was doing psychometry, this meant each person putting a small article in a container. Ivy picked up each article in turn and then gave a reading to the person concerned. At the end she picked up Stan's watch which I had put in, and after giving an accurate description of Stan said, "This person not only says she is a Spiritualist, but is." She then asked to whom the watch belonged.

There have been many accounts of psychic phenomena. Many just want to know about the research side, and have no wish to contact a loved one. They are missing out, as if they did, they would have their own personal proof, making research unnecessary. But it must be a two way thing. If the person in the spirit world doesn't want to contact YOU, there is nothing you can do! This should put a stop to the foolish statements made by Church people who know nothing

160

about this) that a medium can call up anyone in the world of spirit. They have a choice as we have.

Many have their own proof without going to a medium. These are the lucky ones. Maybe they are mediumistic, and if psychic, can, with patience and meditation contact them themselves. It really is necessary though to sit in a good development circle because there is so much to learn. I went on several courses to find out. These were lectures at Stansted Hall. A book I do recommend is 'The Psychic Faculties and Their Development' by Helen Macgregor and Margaret V. Underhill, from the College of Psychic Studies, London. One can also borrow books from their library and attend their lectures. It is essential that one knows the ground work before embarking on any psychic quest. This applies especially to anyone holding a development circle.

It was shortly before I had completed this book that I had heard the sad news that my friend Vivienne had passed away. This was a terrible shock as I never knew she was so ill.

It was her insistence that I write this book, and she also asked me if I would mind including this short poem at the end.

MY OTHER - BETTER HALF

Until you came I was a being - separate- alone;
But within myself there seemed to be
a quantity - of substancy unknown;
I yearned to know - that felt a part of me -
but yet as if another thing - or being.

Was it then my Adam's rib? My spouse in Spirit form?
And were we always one throughout Eternity? Are we affinities?

And this is why, that now you come - in all your ways so sweet -
Fulfilling all my dreams of earthly paradise,
I feel complete - and never more alone.

By Vivienne Cooper

And so - as one door closes - another opens.

CONCLUSION

The spirit world is continually seeking new ways with which to link our two worlds. Since the commencement of this book a machine has come to the attention of the public which caused startling headlines. The machine, called the 'Spiricom' is an electronic machine which, it claims, allows conversations lasting more than an hour with the so-called 'dead.'

Three scientists have made this possible. One a George Mueller, who 'died' in 1967 and whose voice was *recorded* from the spirit world. William O'Neil who built and operated the machine, and has a wide experience of electronics, and last George W. Meek, a Researcher and Industrialist, once a technical staff member of the American Embassy in London. The newspaper 'Psychic News,' dated 24th April 1982, gives this information, 'Scientists Hail Breakthrough in Spirit World Communication.' These three scientists were fully convinced they had established an electronic link with the 'dead' scientist George Mueller after much checking of details given by him from the other side. This machine was developed under the auspices of the Metascience Foundation, based in Athens, California. The news was released to London, Paris, Rome, Zurich, Frankfurt, Tokyo, and Manilla. I did not read it either in the paper, or hear it on television, or the radio. The startling news headlines were in the 'Psychic News' which I read with much interest.

Why were the national press so reticent? No doubt the ridicule they expected to receive would be more than they could bear! The whole thing seemed to be hushed up. I heard no mention of this, when it must have been the greatest story of all time. Even the message from the astronauts on the moon must take second place. Is it too preposterous to imagine a loved one trying with the help of highly evolved spirits to communicate with our world? Have we lost all faith, and is the Bible just a collection of stories much exaggerated?

The Bible is full of spirit communication. The clergy read it but don't believe it; the Bible in other words is Spiritualism at it's best.

Many will say that this machine is not now necessary whilst there are mediums, but that is no answer. Anything or anyone is necessary who has the ability to contact the spirit world. If those first raps in the Fox's home in Hydesville, America in 1848 had been ignored, we would not have known Spiritualism as it is today. It was brought about by two young very psychic sisters, and the raps they heard, made by a discarnate spirit, led to a question and answer discussion between the sisters and the spirit. All planned of course in the spirit world. It was not accepted at first, but gradually attracted large numbers.

Electronic communication was again mentioned in an address by Ernest Thompson, editor of 'Two Worlds' Magazine, which he called, The Future Basis of Spiritualism, which was given to the Newcastle Psychic Research Institute on Sunday 25th January 1948, which is included in this book.

PART TWO

ELECTRONIC COMMUNICATION

THE FUTURE BASIS OF SPIRITUALISM
(AN ADDRESS)
BY ERNEST THOMPSON
(EDITOR OF THE TWO WORLDS)

Given to the Newcastle Psychical Research Institute
Sunday 25th January, 1948.

Published in commemoration of the
Centenary of Spiritualism (1848-1948)

The development of Spiritualism during these last hundred years, as a new Science, Philosophy, Religion, and Social Movement, has a far greater significance and importance for the entire future of Mankind than the majority of Spiritualists realise. It was not an accident that Spiritualism was inaugurated by the Fox sisters in 1848, when the Industrial Revolution was in the process of changing our lives, when Science was rising triumphantly, when the rule of Orthodox Christianity was shaken to its foundations, and when Materialism was rapidly gaining a great influence over the outlook of Man. It was obviously a period of crisis in Man's history. The forces of Materialism spread like a prairie fire, sweeping away the errors and superstitions of orthodoxy from the minds of the people. Reason supplanted Belief. Rationalism alone, however, failed to fill the spiritual void thus created, but gradually the inherent spiritual desires of man slowly re-asserted themselves, and a conscious need for new spiritual values gradually emerged.

As religion has always depended upon the conceptions of a future life and eternal progress, a revelation was needed which would satisfy the new scientific outlook of man by giving demonstrable proof of these truths, and give back to life that purpose for existence which was now completely lacking. 'The Rochester Rappings' owe their fame entirely to the fact that they happened precisely at a period when men were already needing such an opportunity as this incident provided, to investigate the reality of a future life. Spiritualism for this reason is of great significance to the future of the world because of its great accomplishment in uniting science and religion.

Spiritualism is destined, as from its Centenary, to usher in a new "Spiritual Age." To me our Centenary has this historical significance. The "Materialist Age" is now rapidly coming to its close because it has fulfilled its basic function of providing scientific means for completely satisfying man's material needs. The present rapid transition to "World Economy" and "World State" is a manifestation of the fulfilment of Materialism;

A United World State will eventually only require its citizens to labour four hours per day, a development which will provide enormous scope for the spiritual unfoldment of Man. Without spiritual leadership however, Man will rapidly become dissolute and decadent.

That spiritual leadership will be provided, for by that time Spiritualism will have become established as the "Universal Religion" of this planet.

Such, as I see it, is the great calling and destiny of our Movement, and which consequently indicates the enormous responsibility of each one of us to work for this great day

The "Materialist Age" will be supplanted by the "Spiritualist Age" and just as the "Materialist Age" has been a means of uniting man from the isolation of tribalism to "World Citizenship" so it will also be the function of the "Spiritualist Age" to unite the societies of this Material World with those of the Spiritual World, into a new form of Cosmic Society (Cosmocism) The problems and joys, lives and destinies of each spirit, incarnate and discarnate, will be shared interdependently, for the means of communication between the two worlds will have been so improved that *all* people on this earth will have facilities available for them for *perfect* communication with their friends and associates in the Spirit World. This will have been made possible by the discovery of an electronic means of communication which will be entirely independent of human mediumship, thus providing *freedom* of access to a new and vaster world of experience and activity than has ever been experienced by Mankind. Such is the great future of Spiritualism!!

LIMITATIONS OF HUMAN MEDIUMSHIP:

The Future of Spiritualism however will depend entirely upon the progress we make in improving our means of communication between the Spirit World and our own. Spiritualism was founded upon, and has grown from the simple fact that spirits can return and communicate with us through the agency of mediums, thus providing survival after death.

This fact has now been demonstrated over a period of one hundred years (1848-1948). The evidence has undoubtedly accumulated, and the Movement has spread over the entire world. Millions have witnessed demonstrations of survival, and there are very few, if any, who have not heard or read in the press about the claims of Spiritualism.

We would however be super-optimists if we believed that Spiritualism is at present either attracting large numbers into membership or showing signs of assuming "World Spiritual Leadership."

What is holding Spiritualism back? What is obstructing mass acceptance by the public on the one hand and the interest of intellectuals and scientists on the other?

The four chief obstacles are the disturbing complications and difficulties of human mediumship; the decline and depreciation of mediumship; the *relative* disappearance of Home Circles; and the poor standard of so-called "spirit-inspired" mediumistic addresses on Spiritualist platforms.

Spiritualism can have no great future on our present basis of human mediumship. Only a scientifically reliable means of communication, comparable to telephonic and radio communication, can establish Spiritualism as the leading spiritual force in the world!

Before we pass on to a consideration of the possibilities of electronic mediumship let us fully appreciate the numerous limitations of human mediumship.

(a) COMPLICATIONS AND DIFFICULTIES:

I have known Spiritualists, many of whom have been more fortunate than the majority of people in obtaining wonderful evidence of survival, who have, from time to time, revealed that, below the surface, they possessed repressed doubts regarding the reality of survival, because of disturbing elements in the various forms of mediumship which had provided their evidence. Why is this?

One element, which is ever present, is the fact that communications to non-mediums are never entirely direct and first hand. Evidence has been provided in each case by a third person, a medium, and the recipients are placed in the position of having to trust another person for information which is usually of paramount importance to their happiness. They neither see nor hear the spirit whom they once knew and loved. Did the medium obtain the information from their minds? Seldom is the information *entirely* unknown by some living person; and so they wonder.

Even in materialisations, whilst evidence is amply provided by the materialised spirit forms, they are very seldom close likenesses of the discarnate entity claiming to manifest, and the voice and communication, if any, is usually psychologically conditioned by the medium. Even the famous materialisations of Jesus were often unrecognised by his closest friends.

Added to this is the knowledge that our most famous mediums in the past have with one exception, been suspected of fraud, not merely by the general public, but by those in authority in the Movement itself.

Secondly, let us examine the majority of the so-called evidence which is presented to you the public. Ernest Oaten, who has had more experience of mediumship during the last fifty years of Spiritualism than any other living person, has often publicly declared that "seventy-five percent of the so-called mediumship is merely self-delusion, self-hypnotism, and unfortunately in a few cases deliberately fraudulent in character, whilst the remaining twenty-five percent is divided into two categories. Twenty percent could be classed as partial evidence while the remaining five percent is absolutely unassailable in its proof of the continued existence of the spirit." What do we get as a rule? a name, some trivial piece of evidence, e.g.

"You kissed your son's portrait before you came to this meeting," or "You have his photograph in your bag". - and then a very general sort of message, e.g. "You have to keep going on, have no fear, all will be well. God bless you friend."

Your dearest friend may only come to you once or twice in a hundred sittings, but all kinds of unknown and distant friends and relatives some of whom have little in common with you, and belong to a remote period of your life, will manifest much more regularly. One of our most famous mediums has never had evidence of her own parent's survival, after a lifetime of mediumship! Then some evidence will not only contradict the facts of life of the deceased, but will contradict messages supposed to have been given by the same entity, sometimes through the same medium.

Thirdly, mediumship abounds in psychological complications and contradictions. As every communication has to pass through the mind of the medium they have a third party psychological undercurrent. Sometimes due to the difficulty of conditions, a spirit may send his message through a guide and/or intermediary and therefore it loses in originality before it reached the medium. In the deepest trance there is still a psychic link with the sub-conscious regions of the medium's mind, which is never really severed from the body.

In the usual manifestations of trance, and in ordinary clairaudience, the medium's mind definitely conditions and colours the messages received. The medium, however, may pick up telepathically the thoughts and wishes of the sitter, or describe clairvoyantly a thought form of the departed friend the sitter wishes to communicate with, but which has been projected by the sitter himself.

Fourthly, let us consider the problem of telepathic interference. Just as a medium is susceptible to the controlling influence and mental radiations of a spirit, she is also liable to receive intelligence telepathically conveyed by living people. Occasionally a description, and a message has been given by a medium which refers to a person in the body in a distant town!

W.T. Stead was a spirit controlled writer, but occasionally he used to write "spirit messages" from people who were still living, and whose thoughts were transmitted telepathically to him!

All these factors make us appreciate the vast range and possibilities of psychological and psychic processes of which we know very little indeed.

I have enumerated a few of the chief difficulties but combinations of them make mediumship still more problematical. Mediumship at its best is but a groping in a thick fog for an occasional glimpse or a faint echo of a voice. We have to sift the few golden grains from the ore.

(b) DECLINE OF MEDIUMSHIP:

These criticisms are not made to discredit Spiritualism or to indicate that survival is not proven by human mediumship, but simply to get in perspective the power, and limitations of human mediumship so that we can plan, with certainty, the future of Spiritualism.

Personally I do not think that Spiritualism's future progress can be guaranteed with its present foundation of human mediumship, not merely because of the inherent psychological difficulties and unsatisfactory nature of our communications, but also because of an increasingly serious obstacle to the presentation of evidence through human mediumship - our modern social conditions.

It is clear that mediumship today is not to be compared with mediumship of fifty or even twenty years ago. Where are the Homes, Duguids, Hopes and Slades, the Palladinos, d'Esperances, Cooks and Pipers of today?

Again, can we honestly say that, after nearly two thousand years, mediumship is of a higher standard than the wonderful phenomena recorded in the Bible? Still further we know that in even more primitive times mediumship was a very common characteristic of tribal peoples.

What is it that has made such a marked difference in mediumship, especially in the last fifty years? It is the conditions of modern life which oppose psychic development.

When a medium develops she requires conditions in which all factors, such as light, noise and other irritating phenomena, tending to stimulate the conscious mind into activity are eliminated; so that the delicate and high frequencies of spirit sounds and visions may have a chance of percolating into the consciousness. For this reason, the chances of the mediumistic faculty manifesting spontaneously in modern men and women, is becoming more and more remote as the demands of industrial life call for greater and greater conscious concentration of our vision, create more and more noise, and develop a higher state of nervousness as the speed of life accelerates.

Fewer and fewer mediums, with well developed natural gifts, are therefore appearing. Many desire to be mediums but their psychological "make-up" is against their being able to develop into first class sensitives.

Occasionally accidents or illnesses have artificially re-adjusted the psychological relationship between the conscious and sub-conscious minds and produced great mediums. Palladino had an accident as a child which depressed her perietal bone. Mrs. Piper's mediumship followed two internal operations. D.D. Home's mediumship was co-existent with tubercular diathesis, etc., etc.

The average individual however is not mediumistic and generally speaking the psychic faculty is rapidly becoming vestigial in modern civilised people.

(c) DIMINISHING HOME CIRCLES:

Even those who have potential gifts have fewer and fewer opportunities to exercise or develop them because of certain fundamental changes in our family system. It can be said that only fifty years ago family life was centred in the home, and because of this, society was largely characterised by social units - clubs, institutes, societies, trade unions, etc. Nowadays when evening comes, the various members of our families go their separate ways, either to cinemas and dances or to partake of cultural and educational activities in the various social organisations which exist for these purposes.

This modern tendency to live more and more in various forms of social communities whilst having an integrating effect upon the lives of the people generally, and will certainly bring about a greater and more harmonious "Brother-hood of Mankind" has a disintegrating effect upon our family life, because of the greater opportunities and facilities for the development of individual interests and gifts outside of home life. It is therefore not only more difficult to gather regularly as a family circle, but also less probable because of dissimilar interests.

For this reason the opportunities of the spirit people to manifest spontaneously in our homes are decreasing, except in cases where Spiritualists have deliberately organised home circles.

Of course there are a great many circles in existence, but they are proportionately less in number relative to the size of the Movement today. The type of membership of these circles has also changed and usually consists more of friends and associates than of family members.

(d) POOR INSPIRATIONAL SPEAKING:

Finally let us consider the presentation of Spiritualist teachings from our platforms, which is another source of weakness in the Movement. It has been a tradition in Spiritualism during the last hundred years that the speaker should be inspired, or controlled by the spirit people, when expounding the philosophy of Spiritualism. Here again we meet with two very grave difficulties. Demonstrating survival and expounding survival are psychologically contradictory functions.

In order that the ordinary Smiths and Browns of the Spirit World can contact their friends and relatives they require a medium who has little education.

An intellectual medium has a powerful aura, which the Smiths and Browns find very difficult to penetrate. Consequently when the average public medium rises to expound our teachings she provides her controls or inspirers with a brain which cannot successfully negotiate a first class address.

Many of our speakers satisfy the majority of our present audiences, but they do not attract new "thinkers" to our churches. Consequently our Movement lacks a reasonable percentage of first class minds to lead it.

I have realised this most forcibly in trying to find suitable tutors and examiners for our S.N.U. Education Scheme.

A genuine trance address can be very useful, but the majority of our mediums are incapable of genuine trance control. What really happens when they rise to speak is that they suggest (to themselves) spirit control; but actually they only achieve a mild form of self-hypnosis in which they are able to irrupt from their subconscious, their past experiences and a great deal of what they have read in Spiritualist books on their subject. This does not deny a certain amount of spirit influence, but the main content of their addresses arises from personal knowledge.

It is a typical characteristic of a medium that she can boldly stand up to speak f or half an-hour on a subject that she has not even prepared. It is also true that orators, in other walks of life, are either sensitives or mediumistic. Mr. Churchill is a good example.

As the majority of our "so-called" spirit inspired speakers have received little more than an elementary education, it is not surprising that there is a universal outcry, even within the Movement, about the poor standard of our platform philosophy.

Because of this, the very type of workers we need today, the intellectual and the thinker, are repelled from membership even after they have generated an enthusiastic interest in our phenomena.

Trained and educated speakers are therefore essential to our future progress, but with regard to human mediumship I consider that it is no longer capable of providing that dynamic basis for the progress which is absolutely essential to the ultimate triumph of Spiritualism, the final conquest of materialism, the fulfilment of Spiritualism's great mission to mankind, and the establishment of a new "Spiritual Age."

SCIENCE APPROACHES HUMAN WAVE BAND:

Only an entirely reliable and popular means of first hand communication with the Spirit World, free of all the limitations of human mediumship, will bring home the realities of communication with the spirit people, survival after death, the existence of the Spirit World and the conception of eternal progress to the masses of people. Until this is accomplished, the victory and triumph of Spiritualism over Materialism and the establishment of the new "Spiritual Age' will be delayed.

Communication by means of an electronic "Spirit Radio" instrument

175

would achieve this great step forward in human progress. Before we examine this idea in close detail let us review certain recent scientific discoveries which in my opinion, are steps science is taking (unconsciously) towards the production of a sensitive electronic instrument, capable of responding to and translating those ethereal patterns of energy waves, which emanate from the minds of returning spirits, and which contain their thoughts.

When the atom bomb exploded at Hiroshima it not only ended the second World War but proved the existing theories of atomic science concerning the interior structure of the atom. It proved that our first scientific ideas about sub-atomic energy were correct. Sub-atomic energy is the physical borderland between the "Universe of Ether" and the "Universe of Matter."

This sphere of natural phenomena leads to energy frequencies which are beyond the range of the human senses, and opens up a new world of experience, the first adventure in which have caused the scientists to alter their ideas about the laws of Nature.

They realise that the real potential force in matter belongs to an invisible and ethereal order of natural phenomena, and their most recent philosophical reactions are notably in the same direction as the ideas we have held for one hundred years concerning the ethereal world in which spirits live.

The atom bomb has blasted the "iron curtain" between ether and matter and placed the scientists upon a- road of progress which will ultimately lead them to Spiritualism.

Spiritualists are therefore not the only people who are penetrating the veil between the material and the ethereal worlds.

In a different way, with different objectives, scientists are also exploring the invisible universe. John Dalton, of Manchester, was the first scientist to establish the real nature of the ultimate particle of matter - the atom. since his day the scientists have been penetrating the "soul" of the atom and have discovered the electrons and protons, which are not however strictly speaking *material* particles, but forms of energy belonging to the invisible and ethereal spheres of nature. The point is that the study of them will eventually, in my opinion, lead us to the more refined and spiritual forms of energy which are associated with thought.

Theories were put forward regarding the nature and behaviour of these electrons and protons, and their union as neutrons in the atom. The atom bombs has since confirmed these theories to be true!

Scientists have been forced to admit the reality of the invisible and ethereal world which interpenetrates our material world, and they are now proceeding to introduce these new invisible forces into our everyday life.

The recent success of Dr. Thomas' ELECTRONIC BRAIN is but one of the many startling results of Man's new conquests beyond the world of material things. It is of great significance concerning the future of man, and is the most efficient mechanical substitute for a human brain yet invented. Dr. H.A. Thomas has told us that "mass production at the pressing of a button is within sight." There is no industrial process that we cannot do automatically.

He claims that the "Electronic Brain" can solve Britain's economic crisis in a short time, if Government priority were given to its development.

The Americans have already begun to apply the principle; and the flying of an aeroplane across the Atlantic, piloted by an electronic brain, instead of a human brain, marks a new era in electronic research.

The "Brain" will also do such intricate processes as the mass production of complicated machine parts without human aid, detect flaws in silk materials, detect gases in a mine and give warning of their presence. It will detect colour so that the exact shades of dyes can be determined mechanically, and actually INSPECT finished products for size, surface finish, height, composition and colour without human aid.

This means that man is rapidly approaching the final conquest of matter, and will eventually be released from what is now an all-absorbing occupation of material survival. He will soon be placed in a position in which he will be able to turn his attention to the conquest of the practically unexplored universe of spirit and the problems of spiritual survival. Will he? I think he will.

The very process which will finally subdue matter will carry him to the boundaries of the universe of spirit. Furthermore I visualise this Electronic Brain" which will substitute the human brain for the more

177

mundane work of life, as yet another step towards an "Electronic Medium" capable of detecting those finer energies emitted by returning spirits and translating their content into terms of human speech through a loud speaker.

Not only will the "Electronic Brain" lead us towards a "Spiritual Age" but also towards REALLY EFFICIENT AND RELIABLE means of electronic communication with the Spirit World which will unite the two worlds in such a way as will ensure the success of the "Spiritual Age" under the effective and practical leadership of the spirit people.

Spiritual leadership will then become an everyday reality for ALL instead of, at present, a somewhat rare and isolated manifestation with a few outstanding mediums.

As the television set has followed the loudspeakers, so spirit television sets will follow spirit loud-speakers. Imagine what a joy it will be when EVERYBODY will be able to see and speak to their spirit friends regularly. Is this wonderful prospect a possibility? Yes, I think it is. What will make such a wonderful invention possible? The answer may be SUPERSONICS. My theory is as follows. First of all, everyone knows that if you clap your hands once, quickly and loudly in the near vicinity of a large brick wall, the sound thus produced will be reflected by the wall, and you will hear the echo. Suppose a friend is with you, and is standing between you and the brick wall, the friend's body would also reflect a tiny part of this sound back towards you, in a pattern resembling the shape of his form. If however a spirit friend were also standing between yourself and the wall, the spirit would not reflect any of the sound, for material sound would pass through the spirit's etheral body. Why is this?

It is because the low frequency vibrations of the air would find no response in the very high frequency etheral organism of the spirit body.

If however, a sound could be produced, which was of a similar rate of vibration to that of the spirit's body, *it would be reflected.* This sound, of course, would be of such a high pitch that it would be quite beyond our normal hearing capacity. Can man make such sounds? Yes, he can, and more important still, he is already beginning to make practical use of high frequency sound. The science, which deals with this form of research is called supersonics.

Scientists in this country are at the moment experimenting with an instrument which they hope will give "Supersonic Sight" to the blind. This instrument will cause supersonic sound to radiate and reflect a vibrationary picture of what lies before a blind person. A suitable microphone will pick up these sounds, and by means of another device they will give to the blind a form of sense perception which will enable them "to detect obstacles in their path, just like a sighted person, and will be able to walk about freely indoors and outdoors." In other words Man is evolving an auxiliary mode of sight. This principle of detection is similar to the radar process. Now, ordinary human beings are blind to spirit people, but if we could produce supersonics of a similar frequency to that of the ethereal body, we could radiate supersonics of a similar frequency to that of the ethereal body, we could radiate supersonic waves towards the spirit, and devise a means of reception which would convert the reflected ethereal vibrations into amplified electrical impulses which in turn could be translated into light patterns resembling the forms, features, and apparel of our spirit friends.

If the necessary inventions were discovered to make this possible, "Spirit Television" would become an accomplished fact. The central problem, as in "Spirit Radio," is the bridging of the gulf between the low frequencies of matter and the high frequencies of spirit. Meanwhile, however, orthodox science is slowly closing the gap which will some day, little do they know, make the aural reception and vision of our spirit friends as common-place for future generations, as radio and television have now become for us. Needless to say, such a permanent and reliable form of communication between the two worlds will have a mutually transforming and unifying effect upon both forms of society, terrestrial and celestial, with beneficial results such as we can hardly imagine at the moment.

There is a certain amount of evidence to show that our minds can also receive radio waves. On the 14th June, 1946, I published in "The Two Worlds" a report of a seance in Canada during which a medium received, and simultaneously repeated, a radio message from a sinking ship in the Pacific Ocean. The evidence supporting the reality of the medium's experience came next morning, when the disaster was reported in the press. Later I published another interesting case of a high speed professional W.R.N.S. operator, Mrs. Small, of Norwich, who was able to receive, mentally, high speed radio transmission, without the aid of a radio receiver. As such transmissions are conveyed by, and vibrate the ether, and not the air, they are inaudible to the ear, due to their high frequency. This indicates, therefore, that there is some kind of energy link between radio signals and the subconscious mind.

As thought signals can also be received, from spirit people, in the subconscious, this brings us another step forward towards the discovery of radio receiving apparatus, sensitive enough to respond to thought signals. Mrs. Small's experiences suggest that there is some frequency relationship between radio signals and thought signals, in view of the fact that they can both be received by the same human apparatus. What we now have to invent is radio apparatus capable of producing the same results.

Brief mention may also be made of certain other scientific discoveries and inventions which are of importance in research towards "Electronic Mediumship." Obviously radio- and television are our starting points. There is also the invention of radar which is of great significance in so far as Spirit Television is concerned. Electro-encephalographic research is also another milestone on our journey. What is electro-encephalographic research? As most people know, the human brain is a most complex organ and as we use it, when thinking, electrical currents are constantly flowing between the cells. These currents which mirror most intimately its functions can now be recorded by very sensitive instruments, and graphs have been recorded indicating the wave formation of the electrical impulses of the brain under various mental conditions.

ELECTRONIC COMMUNICATION:

The evidence received from the Spirit World is that as we progress, intellectually and spiritually, our spiritual vibrations are correspondingly increased; so that highly developed spirits rise to the higher spheres by a natural process which could be named the LAW OF SPIRITUAL GRAVITATION, whilst more dense and material spirits gravitate to lower and more gross spheres of existence, according to the degree of their spiritual retrogression.

Because of the difference in vibrationary existence, the waves of thought energy will also be of different frequencies, and it might be true to say that two spirits would not be able to transmit their thoughts on exactly the same wave length. This basic fact would constitute the fundamental principle in the construction of what might be termed an "Electronic Medium" "Spirit Radio". Such an instrument would not only have to be sufficiently sensitive to trap the higher frequency band of thought, but would have to be selective, so that different spirits could be tuned into vibrationary range at will. This would leave the control of communications between the two worlds with us. This would not only be fair in view of the fact that, whilst the spirit people are apparently free to visit the earth plane, we are unable, except in very rare instances, to make consciously willed visits to the spirit worlds. There would however, gradually develop mutual co-operation between discarnate and incarnate individuals and societies so that the monopoly would not become a dictatorship.

This arrangement however would ensure that, whilst on the one hand undesirable communicators could be completely barred from forcing their attentions upon us, it would also permit, on the other hand, the highest spirits to communicate with us if we merited such attention. With such a breath-taking revolution in social relationships, the opportunities for spiritual development and progress would be increased a thousand-fold for the people on the earth plane.

The possibilities of broadcasting speeches from great reformers, philosophers, scientists and artists of the past would have inestimable beneficial effects upon our religious ideas, philosophy, science and art.

The fact that spirit radio would eliminate human mediumship would not necessarily put an end to mediumship or the Spiritualist Movement. The radio did not silence the theatre, etc. An artificial mode of seeing and hearing a spirit friend would never equal a personal psychic perception, but it would put an end to the necessity for public demonstrations and private sittings. This new development would not interfere or detract from personal psychic development. In fact there would be an increase in human mediumship because more and more spirits, incarnate and discarnate would be attracted to, and consciously concentrating on "Borderland." On the other hand, there would be an enormous need for teaching and guidance in the new situation thus created.

Obviously great minds would not waste their time in any person's home. Their contact with us would have to be organised on the highest level of co-operation. Meanwhile the new outlook, the new philosophy thus created, would have to be preached, and the new developments brought both into perspective and under leadership.

The scope of the work of the established Spiritualist Movement would be enormously increased. The demand for Spiritualist workers and teachers would be very great. The old regime of human mediumship would, however, have served its purpose, and given place to a greater and higher movement, within which new developments would take place.

The new contact which the individual will acquire with his departed friends and relatives will transform the present attitude of inferiority which some Spiritualists maintain towards the spirit people to one of rational intercourse, and any superiority which they may retain in our minds, will be only that which an incarnate mind would also merit by sheer spiritual or intellectual qualities.

The mysterious mists of death will be finally dispersed and a balanced relationship will replace the pseudo-ghost worship that pervades the darkness of present day seances.

Whilst we can visualise a new movement behind the electronic communication of the future, we must not overlook the fact that a corresponding organisation will spring up simultaneously on the "Other Side" as the new avenues of progress are presented to them. This is precisely what happened one hundred years ago at Hydesville. Higher spirits have very few suitable instruments to use at present, but electronic mediumship would stimulate a new interest in the affairs of their incarnate brothers and sisters on earth. Indeed the necessary research that lies before us will be greatly facilitated, simplified, and speeded up by the spirit people, who will be working on similar lines to our own, with greater knowledge and with equal enthusiasm!

On the other hand let us remember that there is an over-riding intelligence in all such things, which has never allowed man to overstep himself, or called upon him to solve the impossible.

The underlying principle, as I see it, in Electronic Mediumship is the general principle of energy. Energy is simply *matter in motion*. Thought is also energy, but the indications are that the motion of thought is of a very high frequency of vibration.

I visualise thought as originating in the high frequency vibrations of the molecules of memory, which have been created by the electromagnetic energy of sensory perception, and subsequent association mentation, in the unconscious regions of the psyche.

When thought is generated, it stimulates waves of vibrations within the surrounding ether. The electronic instrument must therefore be capable of trapping and conducting these vibrations to where they are required. Perhaps the medium needed for linking up the world of matter and the world of ether may be one of our lightest gases, such as helium, which may respond electro-chemically, conducting through currents to a suitable means of frequency transformation and power amplification by valves, so that the messages could be reproduced at the lower frequency and audibility of normal speech on a loud speaker; just as the radio waves f rom our broadcasting stations are now converted in our existing sets. Spirit television would probably follow a similar process plus those employed in normal television. In order to link up the material and ethereal worlds there must be a common physical basis between them. If the ethereal world were of a different order of nature the problem may never be solved.

Have we any ground for believing that the ethereal and material worlds are indeed merely two aspects of one physical world? Yes, and our authority is none other than Einstein who, in his "Vector Field Theory" affirms that the greatest part of energy is concentrated in matter, but that the field surrounding matter also represents energy in a smaller concentration. The "Vector Field Theory" unites these two conceptions and regards the Universe as a single unified "Field" of energy, in which matter is but a concentrated form, and the Ether of Space a more rarefied form of energy.

The following is a direct quotation from Einstein. "We have two realities: matter and field" (the space surrounding all matter). "Matter is where the concentration of energy is great, field where the concentration of energy is small, the difference between matter and field is a quantitative rather than qualitative one.

There is no sense in regarding matter and field as two qualities quite different from one another. We cannot imagine a definite surface separating distinctly field and matter. In this way a new philosophical background could be created. Its final aim would be the explanation of all events in nature by structure laws valid always and everywhere."

Generally speaking, the picture Einstein has given us is that of a curved field (of ether) existing around every material body, having a material density at any given point inversely proportional to the square of the distance from each respective body. This is in complete harmony with the idea of a Spirit World surrounding our earth in which its members experience relative difficulties as they descend to the more earthly strata of space, because of the increasing contradiction between their higher and more ethereal vibrations and the lower and more material vibrations of the lower spheres of the Spirit World.

What scientific support have we for the idea that thought from spirit to spirit is transmitted as waves of energy across the ether? The greatest scientific support for Spiritualism came from Sir William Crookes who formulated an hypothesis in support of the wave theory.

In his Presidential Address to the British Association for the Advancement of Science, Sir William said: "If telepathy takes place we have two physical facts - the physical change in the brain of A, the suggester and the analogous change in the brain of B, the recipient of the suggestion."

"Between these two physical events there must exist a train of physical causes." He further argues that "with every fresh advance of knowledge it is shown that ether vibrations have powers and attributes abundantly equal to any demand even to the transmission of thought."

He believed that these ether waves are of small amplitude and greater frequency than the X-rays; are continually passing between human brains and arousing a similar image in the second brain to the first, and that the intensity of the waves diminished with the square of distance. The telepathic image, however, may not only be very vivid, despite the remoteness of the agent, but the picture is often modified and symbolical. Hereward Carrington suggests that telepathic manifestations may take place through a superconscious mind, that there may be a meniferous ether, as some writers have suggested, which carries telepathic waves, and that there is a species of spiritual gravitation, uniting life, throughout the universe, as physical gravity binds together all matter.

Such is the scientific knowledge which helps us to prophesy the coming of electronic communication.

TOWARDS THE SPIRITUAL AGE:

I regard therefore the first hundred years of Spiritualist history as the epoch of human mediumship. The results are of two kinds. Our Movement, by demonstrating its phenomena and propagating its teachings, has done an enormous amount of good. It has gradually changed the outlook of the public regarding death and the after-life and the ideas of survival and communication with spirits are gaining ground.

This is reflected in the growing interest in psychic literature, plays, radio broadcasts and films, but the progress we have made and the influence we are creating in society is by no means reflected in our own Movement.

We cannot report any great advance in mediumship, membership, or ideas. In fact our philosophy has sadly strayed from the teachings of the early pioneers. Free interpretation of the Seven Principles has been abused and used as an excuse to import any driftwood from other ideologies and 'isms until Spiritualism has become as sectarian as Christianity. New converts bring orthodox ideas into our services because we make no attempt to teach them our philosophy. Our present policy of collecting all manner of view points together under one banner will only bring disaster.

The longer this continues the greater the amount of explosive material will be collected for ultimate disruption. Human mediumship has aided this process by presenting, through English sensitives, unworthy Eastern philosophies from inferior Eastern races.

Spirit radio will clear up a lot of the misunderstandings which mediumship, through uninformed minds has developed. There will

185

be many objections, and there will be reactionary opposition to electronic mediumship. These objections will mostly overlook the simple fact that electronic mediumship will rid Spiritualism, and communication with departed spirits, of uncertainty, confusion, and fraud. It will be said that communication will lose its spiritual quality; but we must ask ourselves whether mediumship and spirituality are synonymous? It does not follow. Has orthodox religion regarded the radio as a deterrent to the propagation of Christian teachings? On the contrary they have exploited this mechanical form of preaching to the utmost! Some have said "Electronic Communication" will be abused. True, most things have been abused, but we blunder on, and advance in the end. My difficulty is in deciding which side will abuse it most!!

When spirit radios are sold in our shops they will enter millions of homes. The Truths of Spiritualism will become a living reality to al*l* people, all over the world. Everyone's life will be transformed. An outlook based on an existence of three score years and ten will be replaced by the conception of eternal life. The personal emphasis on material survival and security will swing to spiritual values and progress.

The interchange of ideas between terrestial and celestial societies will bring far-reaching changes in our existing forms of society. The past will enrich the present and the future of mankind will hold infinite possibilities.

A new form of Cosmical Society will come into being and will be characterised by the absence of material poverty and war. A new age will begin - "The Spiritual Age".

New leaders will be required to direct mankind along virgin paths of progress and emancipation.

This leadership will fall upon the shoulders of those who are in the vanguard of Spiritualist progress.

Will we be found in the vanguard of Spiritualist progress?

BIBLIOGRAPHY

Newcomers to Spiritualism and Spiritual Healing may be interested in the following books which I have read:-

LOWLANDS OF HEAVEN FROM LIFE BEYOND THE VEIL, Volume I.
By Rev. G. Vale Owen.

HIGHLANDS OF HEAVEN FROM LIFE BEYOND THE VEIL, Volume II.
By Rev. G. Vale Owen.

A VENTURE IN IMMORTALITY.
By David Kennedy.

INTRODUCTION TO SPIRITUALISM.
An Educational Handbook, produced by the Lyceum Department of the Spiritualists' National Union.

LIFE BEGINS AT DEATH.
By Leslie D. Weathermead.

THE PATH OF THE SOUL.
White Eagle Publishing Trust.

SPIRITUAL UNFOLDMENT (i) - About Spiritual Healing.
White Eagle Publishing Trust.

THE PSYCHIC FACULTIES AND THEIR DEVELOPMENT.
By H. MacGregor & M. V. Underhill.

A delightful little book for children - and adults:-

FAIRIES AT WORK AND PLAY.
Observed by Geoffrey Hodson.